Terrance Dicks has written over a hundred children's books, including about sixty in the bestselling series of Dr Who novelizations. He has worked in television as a scriptwriter, was script editor of *Dr Who*, and first script editor, then producer, of the BBC Classic Serial.

Richard Carpenter was an actor for fifteen years before he began writing for television. Among series he has created are *Catweazle*, *The Ghosts of Motley Hall*, *Dick Turpin*, *Smuggler* and *Robin of Sherwood*. *Winjin' Pom* is the first series he has written for puppets.

Winjin' Pom

Written by Terrance Dicks from scripts
by Richard Carpenter

Illustrated by Graham Higgins

Piper Books

First published 1991 by Pan Books Ltd,
Cavaye Place, London SW10 9PG

9 8 7 6 5 4 3 2 1

Text, illustrations and Trademark © Spitting Image
Productions Ltd 1991

ISBN 0 330 32089 0

Phototypeset by Input Typesetting Ltd, London
Printed in England by Clays Ltd, St Ives plc

Winjin' Pom is a Spitting Image production
in association with Central Independent Television

Programme directed by Steve Bendelack
and produced by Marcus Mortimer

Licensed by HIT Licensing Initiatives

Contents

I would like to thank everybody at Spitting Image for their creative contribution to *Winjin' Pom*: in particular Roger Law, Paul Mayhew-Archer, Marcus Mortimer, John Langdon, Steve Bendelack, and finally Scott Brooker, who created the wonderful puppets.

Richard Carpenter

Chapter One

Dirty Work in the Woods

It was a dark and stormy night in the wild, wet woods.

Drenched by a steady downpour, two crows were shoving a battered old camper van into a clearing. In their dark suits, black shirts and white ties, they looked oddly out of place in the open air.

Dirty work was afoot.

'Right, Ronnie?' croaked Reggie Crow, in a voice as richly thick and cockney as a bowl of jellied eels. Reggie was the bright one – relatively speaking.

The relative in question was his brother Ronnie, who was a bit of a thickie. Not that anyone ever said so – at least, not more than once.

Reggie and Ronnie Crow were masters of the underworld – or should that be overworld? From their lair in Trafalgar Square they controlled a mob of streetwise starlings. Every pigeon in the West End paid them protection money.

'Right, Reggie,' said Ronnie, in reply to his brother's enquiry. Ronnie always agreed with everything Reggie said. It was a lot simpler.

Most people always agreed with Reggie, as a matter of fact. It was a lot safer.

'Got the, er, merchandise?' asked Reggie.

'Great!' A lot of Ronnie's answers didn't have much to do with the question.

Reggie frowned. 'Er, Ronnie?'

They heard the wail of a police car siren, uncomfortably close. Instinctively the Crows ducked down.

'Let's go!' snapped Reggie. 'Move it!'

'Right, Reggie.' Obliging as always, Ronnie heaved away at the van.

'Got the merchandise?' asked Reggie.

Reggie watched him despairingly. 'I was referring to *us*, Ronnie, not the van.'

'Oh! Right!'

Reggie hurried off through the woods, and Ronnie followed. They were scarcely out of sight when a pointed face peered around a nearby tree. The face belonged to a ferret called Sid Shifty. Sid sidled from behind the tree. He wore a cloth cap and a shabby duffle coat. One look at his furry features told you he was treacherous, dishonest and deceitful – and that was his good side. Sid peered at the van. There was something written on the side, in big, straggly letters.

Thoughtfully, Sid Shifty read it aloud.

'THE WINJIN' POM.'

Came the dawn.

Came, in rapid succession, the morning and then the afternoon. The rain eased off, the sun shone, just a bit, and an Aussie wallaby came bounding through the woods.

She wore dungarees and a backpack and her name was Adelaide. Behind her trailed Darwin, a fat and bewildered wombat, in dressing gown, slippers and a backpack.

'Frazer!' bellowed Adelaide.

No reply.

Adelaide tried again. 'Bruce!'

'Bruce! Frazer!' piped Darwin huskily.

Still no answer.

Adelaide heaved a sigh that stretched the denim of her dungarees. 'Why'd they have to get off the bus, anyway?' she demanded.

'Bruce went walkabout,' said Darwin, 'so Frazer went after him.'

Adelaide glared impatiently around the woods. 'We've got to get to Windsor by eight tonight. Otherwise we won't get the money – right?' She raised her voice again. '*Bruce!*'

Leaves rattled and birds fell out their nests but there was no reply.

'Half a million pounds!' whispered Darwin reverently.

'Yeah,' said Adelaide sourly. 'And Sydney's gone missing as well!'

3

'What's half a million pounds in dollars?' wondered Darwin.

'I dunno, you're the accountant. *Sydney!*' yelled the wallaby.

Darwin produced a calculator and began tapping its keys. 'Five hundred thousand, divided by five, exchange rate two hundred and fifty to the pound, take off five per cent, add eighteen, that's just enough for the air fare home if we go by train—'

The mumbled calculations broke off abruptly as Adelaide snatched the calculator and shoved it into his mouth.

Well used to Adelaide's little outbreaks of impatience, Darwin removed the calculator, wiped it and tucked it away.

A track-suited, Walkman-wearing rabbit jogged by, muttering, 'Keep fit, keep fit, keep fit . . .'

'Just a mo mate,' called Adelaide. ''Scuse me, have you seen . . .'

'Can't stop. Keep fit, keep fit . . .' Ignoring her, the rabbit jogged straight past them, disappearing into the trees.

'What a peanut!' snarled Adelaide. 'Rack off, ya boofhead!'

'Do you think we're lost?' asked Darwin mournfully.

'I am never lost, Darwin. I have an unerring sense of direction!' Adelaide swung round, strode forwards and bounced off a wooden post. The sign at the top read, 'WINDSOR – 15 miles'.

Just then, in a flurry of amazingly long legs and fluffy feathers, an ostrich arrived on the scene. She wore a frilly dress, a feather boa and a backpack, and carried a fan and that vital ostrich accessory – a red fire-bucket filled with sand.

'Sydney!' cried Darwin delightedly.

But Sydney wasn't happy. 'You promised me culture and castles!' she wailed as soon as she saw them.

Adelaide groaned. 'Ah, don't do yer block, Sydney!'

'Cream teas and Big Ben and Beefeaters!'

'We've only just landed,' soothed Adelaide. 'We'll see everything, once we've collected the money.'

'Mother was right,' sobbed Sydney. 'I should never have left Gullagaloona!'

Adelaide blew her top – again. 'Now listen to me, you arty-farty, high-falutin, feather-brained idiot ostrich . . .'

'*How dare you!*' shrieked Sydney, and plunged her head into her bucket of sand.

'She hates being called an ostrich,' said Darwin.

'She is a flaming ostrich!'

'She says she's a cassowary . . .'

'She's a pain in the pouch,' said Adelaide. Unzipping her own pouch, she produced a folded map, jabbing at it with her finger. 'Windsor's *here* – and we're *here* – in some grotty wood.'

Sydney took her head out of her fire-bucket. 'And how do you know that?'

Adelaide pointed upwards. Nailed to a nearby tree was a wooden sign. 'SOME GROTTY WOOD', it said.

Darwin blinked up at the sign and looked vaguely around. 'Yeah, but Bruce and Frazer are still missing.'

Sydney waved a wing. 'I think they went that way.'

'Then stop flapping yer beak, and let's kick on!'

'Me feet are killing me, Addie,' sighed Darwin.

'Yeah? Well let me know if they need any help!'

Giving her a hurt look, Darwin took off his slipper, sniffed it and keeled over. Recovering himself, he got up and trotted after the others.

Reggie and Ronnie Crow were on their way up.

On their way up in a lift to be precise. It was a once-posh, oak-panelled affair, a bit graffiti-scarred by now. The brass indicator dial read: 'CAR-PARK – HALF-WAY – NEARLY THERE – CROWS NEST'.

As the lift moved jerkily upwards Reggie said, 'Can I ask you something, Ronnie?'

He spoke in the husky, dangerously quiet voice that made every villain in London tremble.

Every villain except Ronnie. He was too dim to be scared.

'Anyfink, Reggie!'

'Where did you nick that motor?'

'Earls Court Road.'

'In a perfect world, Ron,' began Reggie.

'Yeah?' said Ronnie encouragingly.

'In a perfect world, a getaway vehickle should be able to *get away*.'

'Yeah.'

'*Without being pushed*.'

'Oh, yeah!' agreed Ronnie cheerfully.

The lift jolted to a halt and the doors opened on to the Crow's Nest, Ronnie and Reggie's secret lair. High above Trafalgar Square, on the top of Nelson's Column, it was set snugly between Lord Nelson's huge stone feet.

The Crow brothers made their way to the big double desk. Reggie's place was on the right by the answerphone. Ronnie sat on the left where there was a big pile of soft toys. In front of each of the brothers was an identical picture – a big, silver-framed portrait of a white-haired and bespectacled old lady crow.

Since they'd been away from the office on business – dodgy business – the first thing to do was to check the calls. While Ronnie was happily bashing a toy tiger, Reggie flipped the switch. There was a beep and a light, husky voice came from the machine. 'Hallo, Ronnie. Hallo, Reggie . . . it's Andrew Lloyd Webber . . .'

Reggie frowned, then said, 'What, the wally with the theatre?'

'The wally with the theatre,' agreed the voice. 'Look, *please* don't saw the legs off my dancers! Have some free tickets. How would you like to see *Cats*?'

Reggie considered. 'Er, dead!' The line went dead too. 'Creep,' muttered Reggie.

Another beep, another voice, a deep and gritty one this time. 'Ron? Big Kevin here. Say hallo to Reggie for me.'

'Hallo, Reggie,' said Ron obligingly.

'Er, look, I got a problem,' rumbled the voice, with an unconvincing attempt at a light laugh. 'The protection money . . . no can do. Give us a few days, eh? I knew you'd understand.'

Reggie looked across at his brother. 'The boys couldn't have got round there yet, then.'

A crash of broken glass came from the machine, mingled

with screams and the sudden rattle of machine-gun fire. Ronnie pulled the ear off a toy rabbit and tossed it aside. 'That'll be them.'

'Nice one, boys,' said Ronnie.

Another beep, another voice. This one was female. ''Allo, boys, it's your old mum.'

The brothers cringed. 'Oh no, what we done, Mum?'

'Now look,' said the voice sternly. 'If you're thinking of holding up the post office – pop next door and get us a pound of mince. Thanks.'

'Ah, bless her,' said the brothers sentimentally, and each of them gave the maternal portrait a pat and a loving kiss.

'Right,' said Reggie, the rare moment of sentiment over. 'We'd better give Jay Gee a bell. Gimme the stuff.'

'What stuff, Reggie?'

'The stuff we nicked, birdbrain.'

'I thought *you'd* got it!'

'You what?'

Ronnie looked aggrieved. ' "I got the merchandise," you said.'

'No! I didn't say, "I got the merchandise." I said, "Got the merchandise?" '

'Well,' said Ronnie slowly. 'If you ain't got it, and I ain't got it . . .'

The brothers exchanged horrified looks. 'It's still in . . .'

Chapter Two

The Winjin' Pom

'THE WINJIN' POM,' said Darwin slowly. Adelaide, Darwin and Sydney were still hunting for the missing members of their party. They hadn't found them yet, but they'd found the camper, parked in the middle of the woods.

Sydney craned her long neck forward and read out the other slogan painted on the van. 'MELBOURNE OR BUST.'

'Where's Bust?' wondered Darwin.

'It must belong to Aussies,' said Adelaide. She tugged open the rear doors and a cascade of cans tumbled out. Sydney picked up one of the cans. It was a lager can, and it was empty. She sniffed. 'Definitely Aussies!'

There was a sudden clap of thunder followed by an instant drenching downpour. In wild flurry of wings and legs, Sydney shoved her way past the others and into the shelter of the van. Standing outside in the rain, Adelaide said sweetly, 'Sydney dear?'

Sydney peered out. 'Yes, Adelaide?'

'How come they let *two* of you into Noah's Ark?'

Sydney tossed her head indignantly. Adelaide and Darwin clambered after her into the shelter of the van.

They looked around. It was the usual set-up, a tiny metal room with curtained windows, a table and chairs, a tiny kitchen unit . . . The whole place looked as if it had been hit by a bomb. There were half-empty cans, packets and boxes, odd articles of clothing and bits of gear strewn all over the place. Sydney picked up a straw sombrero, fanned herself with it and cast it aside. She picked up a thermos flask, opened it and poured a trickle of still-warm coffee into two plastic cups.

Adelaide took a sip. 'We're running out of time. We've gotta find Bruce and Frazer.'

'Not in this downpour!'

Darwin meanwhile was bumbling around the van, peering about him with an air of bemused interest. He noticed that there was a collapsible double bed built into one wall. He tapped the wall. The collapsible bed collapsed, flattening Darwin beneath it. Adelaide and Sydney turned round at the noise, and saw that a bed had appeared behind them.

'That's handy,' said Adelaide, depositing herself on the bed with a thump.

Sydney sat daintily beside her. She glanced out of the still open door at the driving rain. 'Must be the rainy season here.'

'Ha!' said Adelaide. 'That's the only one they have.'

'How do the Poms stand it?'

'They love it,' said Adelaide. 'Gives 'em something else to moan about, right?'

Sydney looked round. 'Where's Darwin?'

The bed heaved a bit but Darwin was nowhere to be seen.

'You know Darwin's problem, don't you, Syd?' said Adelaide confidentially.

Sydney nodded. 'He lets things get on top of him.'

'Can't take the pressure!'

'Never stands up for himself,' said Sydney. The bed heaved again and Sydney stood up. 'Darwin? Darwin!'

Adelaide stood up as well. The bed slammed back into the wall, revealing Darwin flattened against the underside.

As he slid gently to the floor, Sydney opened a wardrobe cupboard – and jumped back with a squeal of alarm. 'Frazer!'

A goggle-eyed fruit-bat in a black leather jacket and a red polo-necked sweater peered short-sightedly out at them.

'G'day, ladies!' he greeted them.

'You freaky fruit-bat!' shrieked Adelaide. 'What the heck are you doing in there, Frazer?'

'Oh, I'm hanging myself up to dry, as a matter of fact. Rain stopped play, Australia were twenty-five all out, England were five hundred for one . . . Cripes, I must have been having a nightmare!'

'Did you find Bruce?'

'Yep, he's around. Somewhere between silly mid-off and the kitchen cabinet – and on this particular wicket, which, let's not beat about the bush baby is as wet as a wombat's what not . . .'

Leaving Frazer to drone on, Adelaide turned away. 'Bruce! Bruce!' she called.

From around ceiling-level came a high-pitched squeal. '*Geronimo!*'

An eight-legged fur-ball, consisting mainly of school-cap, round spectacles and an enormous mouth, plummeted down on the end of a slender thread. It was Bruce, the schoolboy spider.

'Come on the Red-Backs!' he screamed. 'Right, we done England! Let's shoot through!'

'After we've collected our legacy,' said Sydney firmly.

'Wow!' squeaked Bruce. 'That'll make me a money spider! Going up!' Bruce shot rapidly upwards, chanting, 'Beddings – weddings – mothercare – rubberwear . . .'

'Come back down, Bruce!' ordered Adelaide.

Bruce descended for a moment, gave a loud and fruity raspberry, and shot back up.

'Ignore him,' said Darwin. 'He's over-excited.'

A piping voice floated down from the ceiling.

'There was a young spider from Spain, pushed Grandad under a train . . .'

Sydney shuddered. 'Did we *have* to bring him?'

'Of course we had to bring him,' said Adelaide, outraged. 'He's a member of the club!'

As they stared up disapprovingly at the grinning spider, there was a knock on the side of the camper. Sid Shifty the ferret poked his head inside. Nattily dressed in brown suit, check waistcoat and bright yellow tie, he looked the complete country gent. 'How do all!' he smirked.

'G'day,' chorused the Aussies politely. All except Bruce who swooped down and shrieked, 'Can I bite 'im?'

'No, Bruce!' shouted everyone.

Disappointed, Bruce delivered another fruity raspberry and shot upwards again.

Sid Shifty looked round the little group. 'Don't tell me – you're Aussies!'

Darwin looked amazed. 'How did you know that?'

'Have you been in England long?'

'About two hours,' said Adelaide.

Suckers! Dollar signs clicked up in Sid Shifty's mind.

'We're the Gullagaloona Backpackers Club,' said Adelaide.

'From Gullagaloona,' added Darwin helpfully.

'And we're here to collect a legacy,' said Sydney impressively.

Wealthy suckers! More dollar signs!

'Struck it rich, eh?' Sid said, in a voice positively dripping with warm and sympathetic interest.

Pleased to find a friendly Pom, Adelaide introduced the members of the club.

There was Sydney, the artistic ostrich. She was a dancing teacher back in Gullagaloona, and looked after her old mum. There was Darwin the wombat accountant, Frazer the cricket-mad fruit-bat, and Bruce, schoolboy Red-Back spider and all-round hooligan.

'The Gullagaloona Backpackers Club was founded by Kerry Packhorse the Third, the well-known Australian millionaire,' explained Adelaide.

'He left some of his loot to the present-day club members . . .'

'For a year's luxury world tour,' said Frazer.

'Travelling first class everywhere,' said Darwin.

'And staying in the very *best* hotels!' concluded Sydney triumphantly.

Adelaide looked worriedly at her watch. 'On condition that we claim it—'

'From his lawyer,' interrupted Sydney.

''Cos Kerry's dead, you see,' said Darwin.

'Shut up!' snapped Adelaide. 'The thing is, we have to claim the legacy by eight o'clock tonight, from Kerry's lawyers in Windsor. If we don't make it, the money'll be used to found a home for distressed poodles.'

Sid Shifty opened his coat to reveal a suspiciously large selection of watches pinned to the lining. 'Windsor by eight? You're pushing it!'

'We are?' said Darwin disconsolately.

'What about my camper?'

Sydney looked hopefully at him. 'You'll take us?'

'That'd be plying for hire, darlin'. Couldn't do that. But I could sell it to yer. Only thirty thou!'

Even Darwin could see that thirty thousand pounds for a clapped-out camper was well over the odds. '*How* much?'

'On the clock, old son,' said Sid, realizing he'd gone too far.

Adelaide looked round the van. 'Looks pretty shonky to me – and the outside's covered in graffiti.'

'Graffiti?' protested Sid. 'That's art, that is! Haven't you ever heard of Andy Warthog?' He rapped on the table. 'Fixtures and fittings all included . . .' A roof-screen fell on their heads. '. . . and fully detachable!' said Sid hurriedly. 'Totally waterproof . . .' He tapped the roof with a nearby broom-handle and water poured through. 'And beautifully ventilated!'

Adelaide gave him a beady-eyed stare. 'All right. How much?'

'A grand?'

Sydney stared haughtily down at him. 'A grand?'

'But to you,' said Sid Shifty hurriedly, 'Twenty quid! Er, fair dinkum, eh cobbers?'

'You what?' chorused the baffled Aussies.

'Get you to Windsor,' said Sid temptingly.

'Done!' said Adelaide.

Sid Shifty smiled. 'You could say that . . .'

Considering that the camper wasn't his to sell – he'd found it just after the Crow brothers had abandoned it – Sid Shifty reckoned he'd done quite a good deal.

Far away across the Atlantic, in a city of towering sky-scrapers, it was night. On the top of one gigantic, many-turreted block was a luxurious penthouse. Inside the penthouse, in an incredibly elaborate art-deco office, Howard, a Hawaiian-shirted hyena, lolled on an over-stuffed sofa, toying with a jewelled .45 automatic and babbling happily into the phone. Howard *loved* transatlantic phone calls.

'Oh, but that's wonderful, Reggie. Wonderful! I know

he'll be thrilled, he'll be as happy as Larry. You know Larry? Take it from me, he's a very happy guy! Put you through to Jay Gee? I'd love to, Reggie, but he's in a meeting. Some very important killer whales from Miami . . . So go on, Reggie, tell me again . . . I know, but a fifth time won't hurt. No problems at all? Not even the teeniest weensiest one?'

A burst of organ music interrupted him – Puccini's *Madame Butterfly*. Howard swung round in a panic. 'You're on hold, boys!'

On the other side of the room was a stained-glass screen with an enormous desk in front of it. As the music rose in a crescendo, a Mighty Wurlitzer Organ rose from the floor between desk and screen. Hunched over the pedals was a terrifying figure. As the music died away, the figure swung round, and Howard gulped in terror at the sight of his lord and master.

Scrawny neck, cruel beak, skull-like head with a few wispy feathers and cold, gleaming eyes. Godfather of Godfathers, ruler of a criminal empire that made Ronnie and Reggie Crow's mob look like a kindergarten. This was Jay Gee Chicago, the oldest, the evillest, the richest and the most powerful vulture in the world. On one side of the desk was an elaborate life-support system. On the other side a bank of computer screens gave constant updates on various criminal enterprises. Both sets of instruments were wired to the terrifying figure in the chair.

Jay Gee's voice was a harsh and sinister whisper, like the sound of something decayed being broken in half. 'It bombed at La Scala.'

'Jay Gee?'

'*Madame Butterfly*. The première. Nineteen-oh-four. A flopperoo.'

'Sorry to hear that, Jay Gee.'

'You are a putz, Howard,' said Jay Gee Chicago thoughtfully.

Howard hurried to change the subject. 'I've got the Crow brothers on the line, Jay Gee. *They have the merchandise!*'

'Put 'em on!'

Howard tried to stretch his phone extension to Jay Gee's

chair. It was too short and snapped back like a rubber band. The phone flew back and shattered the glass shade of an art nouveau lamp.

Howard stared at the wrecked lamp in quivering horror.

'I got that lamp from Pavarotti!' croaked Jay Gee.

Howard gave him a terrified smile. 'OK, OK, Pavarotti's. As soon as they open I'll buy you another one!'

Jay Gee sighed and flipped the switch on his speaker phone. 'Hallo, boys, Howard tells me—'

Suddenly all the screens went dead. Jay Gee went rigid and stopped dead too – or almost. With a gasp of horror, Howard ran to the life-support system, unclipped a couple of hand-held heart stimulators, and pumped a few thousand volts into his boss's scrawny body.

Jay Gee jerked convulsively, and came back to life – too rich and too evil to die.

' – you got lucky,' he whispered, completing his sentence.

In faraway London, Reggie and Ronnie were huddled over the phone, in a state of quivering terror. Jay Gee Chicago scared them even more than their old mum – and to make matters worse, they had bad news for him.

Jay Gee listened to their gibbered explanations. 'You left the merchandise in a *what*?'

'In a camper van, Jay Gee,' gabbled Reggie.

There was a horrible snarling hiss, and smoke came from the phone.

'It's well hidden,' added Reggie hurriedly. 'Ain't it, Ronnie?' He held out the phone to his brother.

'Must be,' said Ronnie. 'We can't find it!'

Reggie gave his brother a quick bash on the beak with the phone and snatched it away.

Italian insults sizzled from the receiver.

'Bad line, Jay Gee,' said Reggie hurriedly. 'Er, we're picking the merchandise up tomorrow.'

'*You'll pick it up today!*'

'Yes, Jay Gee,' said Reggie and Ronnie obediently.

The line went dead.

Sid Shifty looked affectionately at the twenty-pound note

and tucked it away. He edged towards the door. 'It's a great little runner, this camper, breaks my heart to let it go.' He pointed. 'Windsor's that way, follow yer nose!' He vanished into the woods.

'What a really nice, helpful little Pom,' said Sydney, flapping her fan.

'Ah, they love us,' said Adelaide.

'It's 'cos we taught 'em to play cricket,' said Frazer. 'Mind you, they haven't quite got the hang of it yet.'

They all crowded into the camper's long front seat and Adelaide switched on the engine.

It turned over with a grumpy snarling sound – but it wouldn't start.

'Come on, get going!' snapped Adelaide.

And a deep throaty voice muttered, 'Get knotted!'

Chapter Three

The Pom Speaks Out

Adelaide stood alone in front of the Winjin' Pom, staring it straight in the headlamps. Somehow she had to get it moving. She peered down at the balding tyres – and heard a sudden squeaking. She looked up, and the squeaking stopped. Slowly Adelaide turned away. Sure enough, the squeaking started. She turned slowly back – and the squeaking carried on. The windscreen wipers were going all by themselves!

What's more, there was something rhythmic about their squeaking. Squeak squeak, squeak squeak squeak squeak squeak *squeak*!

The rotten things were playing 'Colonel Bogey' at her! That Pommy song with the rude words. There was a disgusting farting sound from the exhaust and the wipers stopped.

'Right!' screamed Adelaide. 'Everyone out of the van!'

Nothing happened. Adelaide unzipped her pouch and produced a green loud-hailer with 'Noise Abatement' written on the side.

'EVERYBODY OUT!' she boomed, and the astonished Aussies tumbled out of the van.

'What is it?' asked Sydney.

Adelaide swung round on her. 'WHO PLAYED—' Sydney jumped back with a squawk and Adelaide lowered the loud-hailer. 'Who played "Colonel Bogey" on the wipers?' she demanded.

'What did you say?'

'Those wipers were playing "Colonel Bogey" at me!'

'Yes, dear,' said Sydney nervously.

'Ah, right!' said Adelaide. 'Where's Bruce?'

The schoolboy spider shot down from above. 'Wasn't me!'

'Turned themselves on, did they?'

Darwin bumbled up to her. 'What did?'

'The wipers, the wipers!' Adelaide screamed.

'Addie, would you like a little lie down?'

'Don't humour me, Sydney.'

'Would I, Addie?' asked the ostrich soothingly.

A mad gleam came into Adelaide's eyes. 'Wait a minute – the Pom turned them on by itself!'

Sydney backed away. She looked at the others and moved a finger in little circles at the side of her head. 'Of course it did, dear. Why didn't we think of that, Darwin?'

Adelaide was still muttering to herself. 'The Pom, that's the ticket. It switched them on and it switched them off. On and off! On and off!'

'Yes, dear, of course it did,' said Sydney. She produced a thermometer and slipped it into Adelaide's mouth.

Adelaide snatched it out and tossed it away. 'OK, you drongos – you don't believe me? Watch this!'

Folding her arms Adelaide confronted the van. 'We'll cut our losses, take this clapped-out old lump and dump it on the scrap heap . . .'

Suddenly an angry face appeared on the front of the van. The headlamps became huge bulging eyes and a wide mouth appeared between the front bumpers. The Winjin' Pom was alive – alive and angry. *Right then! I'll see you all in court!* growled a throaty English voice.

Sydney squawked and stuck her head in her bucket of sand. The rest of the Aussies disappeared into the bushes.

'See!' said Adelaide triumphantly.

The Pom's engine was rumbling with indignation. 'I am not staying here to be insulted by a power-crazed kangaroo.'

'Wallaby, you ignorant old banger.'

'Who are you calling an ignorant old banger?'

There was another embarrassing explosion from the Pom's rear end.

'All right,' said the Pom gloomily. 'I'll give you that one!'

'You need an overhaul!'

17

'Have you any idea of the waiting list?' grumbled the Pom. 'I should have gone private years ago.'

'I'll get you going,' promised Adelaide grimly.

'You!'

'We've got to get to Windsor by eight,' said Sydney, popping her head up out of the bushes. 'Otherwise we lose our legacy!'

The Pom sighed. 'Always going on about bleedin' Windsor. Everyone must have got the plot by now!'

Reggie and Ronnie were in the lift, going down.

Ronnie had been thinking – and it wasn't easy. "Ere, Reg?' he said.

'What's up, Ron?'

'What if someone's nicked the camper van?'

'Then "someone" will get welded to the wheel-hubs, Ronnie.'

'Oh, right,' said Ronnie, reassured.

The lift glided downwards.

The Aussies were grouped around the front of the Pom.

'Open up!' said Adelaide briskly.

'No!' rumbled the Pom.

'You heard her,' said Sydney.

The Pom groaned. 'Keep that ruddy ostrich away from me!'

'Don't call me an ostrich!' shrieked Sydney.

'Come on,' insisted Adelaide. 'Open up.'

The Pom's bonnet opened a few inches.

'Wider! *Wider!*'

The bonnet jerked open a bit more and Adelaide peered inside. 'Now cough!'

The Pom gave a rattling cough and there was a clang from its other end. The Pom's eyes bulged in panic. 'Me pipe! I've lost me pipe!'

Adelaide's head was right under the bonnet. A moment later she reappeared. 'Looks bad.'

'What does?' asked the Pom in a worried voice.

'Everything!' She looked hard at the battered Pom. 'You've got a drinking problem, haven't you?'

'I like a drop now and then,' said the Pom uneasily. 'Christmas and that . . .'

'Who are you kidding? I know a heavy drinker when I see one.'

'Leave me alone,' muttered the Pom.

Adelaide was remorseless. 'How much, Pom? How much to the gallon?'

'About five miles . . .'

Sydney gave a little shriek. 'That's shameful!'

'I was driven to it,' groaned the Pom. 'Never 'ad me own garridge. Never known the love of a good driver, or a tender 'and on me big end . . .' He gave a pathetic sob. Encouraged, the Pom went on with the sad tale. 'Got the clamp, twice. Abandoned in Milton Keynes . . . Bought by a gang of Aussies, clattered over every cobblestone in Europe, nicked by two criminal crows – then flogged by a dodgy ferret!'

'Quit winjin', Pom,' said Adelaide. 'Let's have a look at your plugs.'

'My plugs are my business,' said the Pom indignantly.

'Well, I'm making them mine,' snapped Adelaide. 'And they're coming out!'

Reggie and Ronnie were speeding through the countryside in their motor. Like themselves, it was big, black and sinister-looking. It had fins at the back and a golden crow on the front. At least, they were trying to speed. Unfortunately, a slow-moving old truck, the property of the Sam 'n Ella Egg Company, was blocking the narrow lane ahead of them.

In the front passenger seat, Reggie was growing a mite impatient. He turned to Ronnie, who was at the wheel. 'Strategic plan B, I think, Ronnie.'

'Right!' said Ronnie, obliging as ever. 'Er, what's that, then?'

'Hit him!'

'Right!' Ronnie put his foot down, and the big black car surged forward, giving the lorry ahead a bump which sent it spinning off the road. Egg boxes flew in all directions,

'Let's have a look at your plugs.'

leaving a trail of eggy debris, and the lorry ended up on its side in a ditch.

Ronnie accelerated smoothly past the wreckage. 'All right, Reggie?'

'That's the sort of thing I mean, Ronnie.'

The black car sped on its way.

The Aussies were gathered round the cringing Winjin' Pom, like a top surgical team in a hospital soap opera.

Adelaide was playing Doctor Kildare. 'Spanner!' she barked.

'Spanner,' said Darwin, passing the instrument over.

Adelaide rummaged inside the Pom's open bonnet, producing moans and groans of complaint.

'Screwdriver!' Sydney came forward with the screwdriver.

More poking about, then, 'Hammer!'

'Spanner,' said Darwin, eagerly producing the wrong tool.

'Dill brain!' snarled Adelaide. 'Hammer!'

Darwin found the hammer and handed it over.

More banging about, more moans and groans from the Pom.

'Hacksaw!' said Adelaide finally.

'No!' yelled the Pom. 'Not that! Anything but that!'

Adelaide mopped her brow and began sawing away.

'Oh, the pain, the pain!' bellowed the Pom. 'Anyone else'd get an anaesthetic.'

'Anaesthetic!' called Adelaide.

'Hammer!' said Darwin, passing it over.

Adelaide delivered a tremendous wallop.

'Thank you,' moaned the Pom, as everything went black . . .

When the operation was over, Adelaide emerged from the Pom's innards. 'Something to stick him back together with!'

Darwin, who was chomping away steadily, said, 'Chewing gum?' He untangled a well-chewed lump of gum from his teeth and handed it over. Adelaide plunged back inside the Pom.

Frazer and Bruce were waiting inside the camper.

'I don't feel too clever, Frazer,' complained Bruce. 'I think I'm gonna chuck up!'

Frazer tried to distract him. 'Eye on the ball, Brucie! Any brothers and sisters?'

'Yeah, three hundred and eighty-five, actually.'

'And you never really knew your dad, did you?'

'No, he died before I was born.'

'Oh, I didn't know that. Bit of a bouncer, eh, Brucie? Still, I bet your mother loved him very much.'

'I know she did,' said Bruce cheerfully. 'That's why she flaming ate him!'

Adelaide slammed down the Pom's bonnet and stood back. 'Well, I've done all I can. The rest is up to him. I'm afraid he's still not fit to drive.'

'Who says I ain't,' rumbled a deep, grumbly voice. The Winjin' Pom was awake.

The Aussies piled inside and Adelaide settled herself behind the wheel. She looked at the dashboard clock. Seven-thirty.

'Strewth! We've only got half an hour to get to Windsor!' She pressed the starter. The engine turned over sluggishly then packed up.

'Somefink tells me you ain't gonna make it!' said the Pom. 'Hur, hur, hur!'

Chapter Four

The Pom Takes Off

'Next left, Ronnie,' said Reggie.

'Right, Reggie.'

'No, left, Ronnie.'

'But you said —'

Reggie sighed. 'Don't start.' He pointed. '*That* way . . .'

The car turned sharp left, smashed through a five-barred gate, and disappeared down the narrow lane that led to the woods.

Crowded into the Pom's front seat, the Aussies tried to goad the reluctant vehicle into life.

'Start, you rust-riddled write-off!' commanded Adelaide.

The Pom groaned. 'I've got metal fatigue.'

'*I'll give you metal* — ' Adelaide controlled herself with a mighty effort. 'Now come on, Pom,' she cajoled. 'Shut your eyes and think of England!'

'If he does *that* he'll never start,' said Sydney despairingly.

The Crow brothers reached the end of the lane – and saw the Pom. Ronnie zoomed up right behind the old camper and screeched to a halt. Reggie and Ronnie climbed out of their car and lumbered towards the van.

Suddenly the Winjin' Pom roared into life. For a moment it vibrated furiously. Then, with an extremely vulgar farting sound, a cloud of black smoke shot out of the newly repaired exhaust pipe. Leaving the Crow brothers coughing and choking behind it, the Pom shot off like a rocket.

'After it!' roared Reggie.

The Crow brothers jumped back in their car and the chase was on! Unaware, for the moment, that they were being chased by two dangerous criminal crows, the Aussies trundled happily along.

Squeezed up between Frazer and Adelaide, Sydney

fanned herself delicately. 'Oh to be in England, now that April's here!' she sang.

Bruce dropped down suddenly from above. 'As long as it isn't Sunday, and you don't have to drink warm beer!' With a mad giggle, he shot upwards again.

The Pom turned on to the main road and speeded up. Minutes later, the Crows' black car burst through a hedge on to the road – to find the Pom just ahead.

'There it is!' yelled Reggie.

'We've got 'em!' shouted Ron.

Suddenly the Aussies saw a road sign. 'Windsor!' they shouted happily, and they all cheered.

A sinister-looking black limo drew alongside.

'Gordon Bennet!' said the Pom. 'It's the Crows!'

'The Crows?' said Sydney loftily. 'Who are the Crows?'

'Lunch!' piped Bruce happily. 'Can I bite 'em?'

'Pull over, you old bag!' yelled Reggie.

'Get stuffed!' shouted Adelaide.

Sydney peered disdainfully down at the Crows. 'Don't you have any manners?'

Ronnie patted his pockets. 'No, I left them at home.'

Sydney craned her long neck through the Crows' window. 'I suggest you apologize immediately.'

'Shut it, you 'orrible ostrich,' snarled Reggie.

'I'm a cassowary!'

Ronnie reached up and grabbed Sydney's beak, and for a moment the two vehicles sped along side by side, linked by Sydney's neck – which stretched as they veered apart.

Ronnie let go of Sydney's beak, and her head spanged back.

'Pull over!' ordered Reggie again.

'You're blocking the road, mate!' said Adelaide severely.

'Do you hear that, Ronnie?' said Reggie. 'We're blocking the road.'

'Right, Reggie,' said Ronnie obediently.

He zoomed past the Pom, and then swung the big, black car sideways across the road.

The Pom zoomed towards the barrier of the Crows' limousine.

Sydney buried her head in her fire-bucket. Darwin pulled

his dressing gown over his head. Frazer's eyes bulged even wider in horror and Bruce disappeared towards the roof.

'The brakes, Pom, the brakes!' screamed Adelaide.

'Wot brakes?' growled the Pom.

The Aussies closed their eyes and prepared for the end. But the Pom had more tricks than they knew.

Suddenly it took off like a show-jumper, and sailed clear over the astonished Crows and their car, drenching them with sludgy black oil as it roared overhead.

Landing back on the road with a bone-shaking crash, the Pom disappeared in the direction of Windsor.

Sydney took her head out of her bucket and the others opened their eyes.

'He – jumped it!' gasped Adelaide.

'Nothing like gravity to bring you down,' said the Pom gloomily.

They trundled on their way.

The stunned Crows meanwhile were sitting in semi-darkness behind their oil-blackened windscreen.

'Don't just sit there, Ronnie,' gasped Reggie, starting the windscreen-wipers. 'Step on the gas!'

'I can't see any gas, Reggie,' protested Ronnie. 'There's too many pedals down there.'

'Ronnie,' said Reggie gently. 'Have you ever had your brains blown out by a squadron of light aircraft?'

Ronnie loved quizzes.

'Er, wait a minute, don't tell me . . . no?'

After a brief drive through the quaint old town of Windsor, the Pom pulled up outside a handsome old Georgian house. The brass plate on the door read *Catchpole, Shyster & Pettifog – Solicitors*.

'Five to eight – we made it!' shouted Adelaide exultantly.

'I'm knackered,' groaned the Pom.

The Aussies piled out of the van, and Adelaide banged the brass door-knocker. A window slid upwards, and a cross-looking hedgehog peered down at them over its glasses. 'Yes?'

'We're the Gullagaloona Backpackers,' called Adelaide.

'From Gullagaloona,' added the ever-helpful Darwin.

'We're closed,' droned the hedgehog and slammed down the window.

Adelaide hammered on the door, the window reopened and the hedgehog peered out. 'Yes?'

'We've come to claim our legacy,' explained Adelaide.

'You should have been here by eight!'

'It is eight!' yelled Adelaide.

The hedgehog shook its head. 'It is five minutes past eight, madam.' The window slammed down.

'It can't be!' screamed Sydney. 'It just can't be!'

Adelaide hurled herself back into the Pom's cab and tapped the dashboard clock – which promptly sprang out of the dashboard.

'Well, it's like the rest of me,' said the Winjin' Pom defensively. 'Runs a bit slow . . .'

The enraged Aussies hurled themselves on the Pom, belabouring it and shouting abuse.

'You four-wheeled nightmare!' shouted Sydney.

'You malingering hypochondriac!' screeched Adelaide.

Even the gentle Darwin said sorrowfully, 'You're a *bad* Pom.'

'I'll smash you to pieces,' hissed Frazer.

'I'll bite your tyres to bits,' threatened Bruce.

'You evil-minded old vehicle!' sobbed Sydney.

'You two-litre layabout,' shouted Adelaide.

The Pom's battered old face crumpled as if it was about to cry.

'Now hold it!' said Frazer. 'We may have lost the innings but we haven't lost the match. We can still tour the world.'

Darwin was baffled. 'Without the money?'

'Sure, Darwin, no worries.'

'Don't be absurd!' said Sydney loftily.

'Maybe it isn't so absurd,' said Adelaide slowly.

Darwin frowned. 'But where would we stay?'

'We can live in the Pom!' said Adelaide triumphantly.

Sydney drew herself up. 'A year? In this – this *bog-wagon*?'

'Sydney!' said the others in a shocked chorus.

The Pom was offended too. 'Yeah, you mind your language.'

'It's better than nothing,' said Adelaide.

'Yeah – and it's ours,' said Darwin.

('That's what you think,' muttered the Pom.)

Adelaide rallied her troops. 'We're Aussies, aren't we? What do you say? Today, Pommyland – tomorrow, the world!'

'Anne Hathaway's Apartment,' sighed Sydney.

'The Thames Barrier Reef,' mused Darwin.

'The Hanging Gardens of Basildon,' whispered Frazer.

'No thanks!' said the Pom firmly.

Darwin stroked the old camper's battered bonnet. 'Come on, Pom!'

'Please!' chorused the others.

'Well . . . Promise not to give me a hard time?'

The Aussies all nodded eagerly.

'Oh well,' grumbled the Winjin' Pom. 'In that case – yes! I mean, I had to say yes, didn't I – or we'll never get this show on the road!'

Chapter Five

It's a Record!

The Winjin' Pom was trundling along a quiet country road. Adelaide was at the wheel. 'This ain't the way to London,' she complained.

'We're not going to London,' rumbled the Pom.

'Who sez?'

'I sez.'

'I'm the driver!'

'And I'm the motor – and I say we gotta get away from the Crows.'

By now the Crows had managed to get the oil off their windscreen. The big, black car was zooming along another lane not far away. Ronnie, as usual, was at the wheel.

Reggie glared angrily down the empty road ahead. 'It would appear you've lost 'em, Ronnie!'

'Have I, Reggie?'

Reggie sighed. 'You know, if they gave a prize for cock-ups, you'd leave it on the bus.'

'Would I, Reggie?'

The Pom spotted an open gate, turned sharp right, and came to a sudden halt in a field behind a hedge. Jolted by the stop, the Aussies looked at each other in alarm.

'Why've we stopped?' asked Darwin.

'I'll ask him,' said Adelaide. She climbed out of the cab and went round to the front of the Pom. 'What are you playing at?'

'I'm hiding, ain't I? From the Crows.'

'Why?'

A cunning look came into the Pom's bulging eyes. 'You got something they want.'

'And what's that?'

'Me!'

'Why would anyone want you – ya grotty old banger?'

'That's nice, that is,' grumbled the Pom. 'That's really nice. I'll have you know I was their getaway vehicle. And what is more, *I still got the loot!*'

Adelaide looked thoughtfully at him for a moment – and changed her tone. 'Winj, old sport, old chum, old darling – where exactly is this loot?'

'Search me!'

'Too right I will!' Adelaide dived back inside the van.

The Crows still hadn't found the camper – though by now they were much nearer then they realized.

'I'm worried, Ronnie,' said Reggie. 'What if Jay Gee susses us?'

'How's he gonna do that then?'

The car-phone rang and Ronnie picked it up. 'Yeah? Oh, 'allo, Jay Gee!'

Realizing what his brother had just said, Ronnie squawked, 'It's Jay Gee! Aaaargh!' and drove the car straight into a hedge.

Since Reggie and Ronnie regarded seat-belts as being sissy, their beaks went straight through the windscreen. Surrounded by shattered glass, Ronnie was still clutching the phone. 'Er . . . we was just talking about you, Jay Gee!'

The sound of the crash brought the Aussies tumbling out of the van. Sydney stretched her long neck and peered over the hedge. On the other side, just a little way along, a big, black car was jammed bonnet-first into the hedge. Through its shattered windscreen she could see two sinister black-suited figures.

Sydney ducked down. 'It's them! It's the Crows!'

Adelaide turned to the Pom. 'Pretend you're a tractor!'

Reggie snatched the phone from his brother. 'You dozy prat!'

In his ear he heard Jay Gee Chicago's sinister whisper. 'Whaaat?'

'Er, cosy chat!' gabbled Reggie desperately. 'Time we 'ad one, right, Jay Gee?'

'OK,' said Jay Gee. 'So where's the merchandise?'

'Well, to be perfectly honest — ' began Reggie.

'We lost it!' said Ronnie helpfully.

'Now listen, my friends,' hissed Jay Gee. 'If that gizmo ain't in my possession by tomorrow – the Crow brothers are history!'

Reggie stared at the phone in horror. 'Jay Gee says we're history!'

Ronnie frowned. 'We didn't do history at our school. Couldn't we be geography?'

Behind the hedge, Adelaide and Darwin were eavesdropping. 'What a peanut!' whispered Adelaide.

Knocking the rest of the glass from the windscreen Reggie said, 'OK, Ron, move it!'

The Crows' car sped away.

'They've gone!' said Adelaide, straightening up. 'Come on, let's search the Pom for the loot.'

The Aussies ransacked the Pom from top to bottom without success.

'What exactly are we looking for?' asked Darwin.

'We don't know,' said Adelaide. 'But we gotta find it before the Crows find us!'

Only Frazer the fruit-bat took no part in the search, settling down in a corner for a quiet banana. Bruce the spider dropped from the ceiling and dangled in front of him. 'Wanna pop me zits, Frazer?'

'Think I'll take a rain-check on that one, Brucie.'

'What are they all up to, Frazer?'

'Most likely lost the ball, Brucie. I remember once at Lord's, in seventy-eight I think it was . . .'

'They ain't playing cricket,' objected Bruce.

'No . . . they weren't doing much of that at Lord's, either.'

Frazer chuckled. 'Funny little place, England. What do you think of it so far?'

'Too many Poms.'

'Fair suck on the sherbet, Brucie. They gotta live somewhere.'

'Why?'

''Cos we don't want 'em all coming to Oz!'

The search was still going on without much result – until Darwin fell over a flat, square, wooden box, heavily padlocked, which had been hidden under the table.

Darwin plonked the box on the table, then picked up a pencil which had rolled beside it. 'Aaah, I found it!'

They all looked at the mysterious box – all except Darwin, who was happily absorbed with his pencil. 'My favourite pencil. Dropped it this morning . . .' He sucked the end. 'Tastes even better.' He scribbled a few words. 'Doesn't spell any better, though . . .'

Ignoring him, the others crowded round the box. Adelaide unzipped her pouch and produced a mallet, a first-aid box, a portable radio . . .

'You seem to have everything but the kitchen sink!' exclaimed Sydney.

'Never know what you might need in Pommyland,' said Adelaide, producing a small kitchen sink. 'Ah, here we are!' She came up with a huge bunch of keys. She selected a key, put it in the padlock and turned it. The padlock opened.

Darwin was impressed. 'How did you know which key to use?'

'Dramatic licence!'

Adelaide opened the box. It proved to be a velvet-lined case. Nestling inside was a dusty old 78 record.

'It's just an old record,' said Darwin.

'Really, Darwin?' said Adelaide witheringly. 'I thought it was a toilet seat.' She read the faded label. '*Nellie Melba . . . Nineteen hundred and six . . . They call me Mimi*.'

'Why do they do that, Adelaide?' asked Darwin.

'Mimi!' said Sydney ecstatically. '*La Bohème*!' She raised her voice in song. '*They call me Mimi*!'

Darwin was amazed. 'You too, Sydney?'

'My favourite,' sighed Sydney.

Adelaide scowled. 'Your favourite what?'

'Opera, opera!'

'We all fall down!' piped Bruce, zooming down from the ceiling.

'She was the greatest Australian singer of them all,' said Sydney, with a haughty flourish of her long eyelashes.

'Aww, turn it up,' said Bruce. 'She ain't even in the charts.'

'I've found it!' said Darwin.

Sydney said scornfully, 'She's dead, you ignorant little sprog!'

'Never stopped Elvis,' said Bruce irrepressibly. Delivering a magnificent raspberry, he shot upwards again.

Adelaide scratched her head. 'Who'd want a scratched old 78?'

Some time later, in a quiet little country town, the Winjin' Pom screeched to a halt outside a solid old Gothic mansion, rear-ending the white police car parked outside. Over the door of the house were engraved the words – COP SHOP.

After quite a bit of argument, Adelaide had convinced the others that they must hand over the stolen goods to the law.

Inside the police station, their arrival had been observed. The desk sergeant, a stout old pig called Sergeant Hog, raised his voice. 'Porker!'

Immediately PC Porker, a plump, bespectacled young pig, appeared at his side. 'Sarge?'

'Porker, there's a very subversive-looking camper outside. I don't like the look of it.'

'Right then, I'll clamp it, Sarge.'

'All our clamps have been nicked,' said the Sergeant sadly.

Adelaide and Sydney came marching boldly into the station, trailed by Darwin who was clutching the flat box.

Before they could say anything, Sergeant Hog grunted fiercely, 'Who owns that vehicle?'

'She does!' said Darwin and Sydney, indicating Adelaide.

'No, we all do,' protested Adelaide.

'You see, it was used in a robbery,' said Darwin confidentially.

'Sounds like a confession to me, Sarge,' said PC Porker alertly.

Adelaide took the box and plonked it on the counter.

'*This* is stolen property!'

'An admission of guilt!' said PC Porker excitedly.

Sergeant Hog said sternly, 'You're admitting this crime, are you?'

Sydney waved her fan in the general direction of the Pom. 'That was the getaway vehicle!'

'Oh, was it?'

'Well, that's what the camper told us,' said Darwin.

'You drongo!' hissed Adelaide, delivering an elbow-jab that doubled Darwin up.

'Oh, I see,' said Sergeant Hog ponderously. 'Your camper talks, does it?'

'Well, in a way, Sergeant, it does,' said Sydney.

'Don't you get whimsical with me, madam,' snorted Hog. 'Porker – breathalysers!'

'Right away, Sarge!'

'Now just a minute, sport!' said Adelaide menacingly.

'Threatening behaviour, Sarge,' said PC Porker happily.

Adelaide clenched her fists. 'I'll drop you, you ignorant fascist scumbag!'

Sergeant Hog tried to grab her, and Adelaide thumped him – then nutted him to be on the safe side. Suddenly the whole cop shop was in pandemonium. Sydney and PC Porker were engaged in a kind of duel, fan against truncheon. Adelaide and Hog were grappling furiously. Darwin cowered in a corner close by, trying to keep his head down. Frazer wandered in and surveyed the scene with amazement. Using his banana as a microphone, he delivered a cricket-style commentary. 'Yes, an interesting day's cricket. There seems to be a little discussion on the pitch, Darwin's reluctant to go . . .' A savage swipe from Sydney's fan missed Porker entirely and clobbered Darwin instead. As Darwin sank slowly to the floor, Frazer continued, 'Yes, Darwin's retiring hurt, bit of a bouncer, that!'

Battling valiantly, Adelaide and Sydney were finally overcome, and Darwin recovered just in time to surrender. Frazer concluded, 'Well, it looks as if the lunchtime scoreboard shows England winning – by two falls and a submission.'

Sadly, Frazer slipped away. A bad result for the Aussie team – something ought to be done about it. Maybe little Brucie would have some ideas . . .

*

The Aussies were behind bars, down below in the police station's old-fashioned cells.

'Me, in jail – the disgrace!' said Sydney tragically. 'It'll kill mother! And you're to blame, Adelaide, hitting that policeman . . .'

'You gutless bush turkey – I wanted to hit him.'

'Look where it's got us!'

'No worries,' said Adelaide confidently. 'We ain't staying.'

She unzipped her pouch, produced her hacksaw and started sawing at one of the bars.

Darwin looked on sadly. The bars were very thick, and there seemed to be an awful lot of them. 'There must be some other way.'

Adelaide went on filing. 'You got dynamite?'

Darwin sighed. 'No, only a pencil.'

Upstairs in the station, PC Porker was quietly reading the *Sun*, while Sergeant Hog walloped him over the head with a selection of truncheons, each one bigger than the last.

PC Porker ignored most of the blows, but after the latest wallop from the biggest truncheon he looked up from his paper and frowned. 'I think I felt that one, Sarge.'

'Right, Constable, I'll order a dozen.' Sergeant Hog started filling in a form and PC Porker returned to his paper. Neither of them noticed a policeman's helmet sliding stealthily across the floor. After a moment the helmet tilted up, revealing a school cap and two big bespectacled eyes. There was a maniacal giggle, and the helmet lowered and slid on its way.

'Psst!'

Adelaide looked up at Sydney. 'Did you psst?'

'Why should I? I've got nothing to psst about.'

'Psst!'

Darwin looked up. 'Well, somebody psst.'

'Stand by your beds!' piped a familiar voice.

'Brucie!' said Adelaide.

'The one and only.' By now Bruce was dangling in front of the bars. 'Staying long?'

Sydney tossed her head. 'If you've simply come to gloat . . .'

Bruce giggled. 'Ah, the first ten years are the worst!' Adelaide waved her fist at him. 'Listen, you nasty little — '

'You better be polite to little Brucie – or I'll just choof off back to Oz and do nothing for you,' threatened the spider. He yo-yo'd excitedly up and down. 'I got a plan to get you out of here. It's a piece of cake!'

'Hope it's got a file in it,' said Darwin.

'Thank you, Birdbrain of Alcatraz,' said Adelaide bitterly. 'All right, Brucie, you're our only hope. What's the plan?'

Chapter Six

The Record Breakers

PC Porker plodded back into the police station. 'Nothin' incriminating in the van, Sarge.'

'Use your head, Porker,' said Sergeant Hog wearily.

'I tried, but I couldn't quite get it off. How about planting some of those stolen tellys?'

The Sergeant looked shocked. 'I couldn't do that! I'm saving them for the Christmas raffle.'

PC Porker didn't seem to be listening. He was staring in horror at a point just above the sergeant's head.

'What are you lookin' at?' demanded Hog.

From above Hog's head, a piping little voice answered, 'Me!'

What Porker could see and Hog couldn't was Bruce, dangling inches above the sergeant's head. 'It's a spider, Sarge. The deadly Australian Red-Back! One bite and you're done for . . .'

Suddenly Hog felt the patter of tiny feet on his scalp-bristles.

'The Eagle has landed!' squeaked the sinister voice. 'One small step for mankind, and eight for little Brucie!'

Instinctively, Sergeant Hog stood up.

'Siddown, fatty!' commanded the voice. 'I gotcha covered – one move and you're lunch!'

Hog sat down. 'Don't move, Porker,' he whispered.

Porker fidgeted. 'Permission to scratch my—'

'No!'

'What's yer name, fatty?' asked the voice on his head.

'No, it's not fatty, it's Sergeant Hog.'

Bruce gave one of his mad little giggles. 'Haven't I seen you at a barbecue, hiding under the apple sauce?'

'Do something, Porker!' pleaded Sergeant Hog.

'Do something, Porker!' pleaded Sergeant Hog.

Porker gulped. 'Permission to remain totally inactive, Sarge?'

Bruce dabbled his feet on the Sergeant's sweating scalp. 'Aw, your head's getting all slippery. Self-basting, are you? Hey, you are listening, aintcha?'

'I'm listening, I'm listening!' quavered Hog.

'Then give yer keys to bacon-bonce here.'

Hog fumbled a big bunch of keys from his pocket and passed them over to Porker.

'Now then, you go and let me mates out, OK?'

'OK, OK!' Porker trotted away.

Bruce rolled his eyes towards the window, where Frazer was hanging upside down, observing with interest. 'How'm I doing, Fraze?'

'A marvellous delivery, Brucie!' said Frazer happily. 'The opposing batsmen clean bowled, and Australia takes the lead!'

Down below in the cells, PC Porker released the Aussies.

'What's going on?' asked Adelaide.

'Some terrorist is holding the Sergeant hostage.'

'So we're free?'

'As a bird, madam.'

Sydney shoved him into the cell and slammed the door. 'Cassowary, *if* you don't mind!'

They hurried up the stairs and through the police station, where Bruce was still perched on the trembling Hog.

Adelaide snatched up the padlocked record-case and passed it to Darwin. 'There could be a reward for this.'

'No worries,' said Darwin. 'It'll be safe with—' He slipped, disappeared from view, popped back up again, still clutching the case. 'Me!' he concluded triumphantly, following Adelaide and Sydney from the station.

Bruce bounded from the sergeant's head to the ledge of the open window. 'Up the Red-Backs,' he jeered. 'Grow your own dope – plant a Pom!' With a last crazy giggle he vanished.

Free at last, Sergeant Hog leaped to his feet. 'Porker! It's truncheon time!'

From down in the cells came a hollow groan.

Reunited, the Aussies piled back into the camper.

'Come on, Pom!' urged Adelaide, and for once the Pom came through. It zoomed forwards, gave the parked cop car a farewell bash, reversed rapidly, turned and disappeared over the horizon in a cloud of oily black smoke.

'What's the blooming hurry?' grumbled the Pom as they sped through the country lanes. 'I mean, I hate to sound negative, but I don't see why I should blow my gaskets just because you lot—'

'All right, all right,' said Adelaide. 'We can risk a bit of a rest.' She pulled into a quiet lay-by.

Minutes later a long black car coasted silently up behind them. The Crows got out, and crept silently towards the camper.

Sydney looked out at the rolling countryside and fluttered her fan. 'We're fugitives! Fugitives!'

Darwin nodded sadly. 'Lost in the wilds of – where are we?'

'England, ya drongo,' said Adelaide.

'We might as well be in Outer Mongolia,' said Darwin sadly.

Adelaide chuckled. 'Outer *Pom*golia, you mean!'

'Let's have a nice cup of tea,' suggested Sydney.

'One lump or two?' asked Reggie Crow politely, shoving a machine pistol in Adelaide's ear.

'Or would you prefer a sweetener?' asked Ronnie, brandishing another pistol.

Sydney screamed and ducked her head into her firebucket. The triumphant Crows surveyed their captives.

'You people have caused us a lot of aggro,' said Reggie with sinister softness. 'Now, where's the welly?'

Like all proper cockney criminals, the Crows used a lot of rhyming slang.

Adelaide looked blank. 'Welly?'

'The welly boot,' said Reggie.

'Loot!' explained Ronnie.

'Yeah,' said Reggie. 'Hand over the pie and mash!'

'Stash!' said Ronnie.

Adelaide played for time. 'What stash?'

'You know,' said Ronnie. 'The nicely!'

'The nicely?' chorused the baffled Aussies.

'The nicely painted china plate,' said Reggie impatiently.

Frazer popped his head through the cab's rear curtain.

'The Nellie Melba 78!' He found himself peering down the barrel of Ronnie's pistol and vanished with a terrified squawk.

'Oh, all right,' grumbled Darwin. Bending down he took the record case from under his feet and handed it over.

As Reggie snatched the case, Adelaide asked, 'Just out of curiosity – where did you get that?'

'Ah, now that'd be telling,' said Reggie slyly.

'No, Reg,' said Ronnie patiently. 'Saying we nicked it from Studmare Hall – *that'd* be telling.'

The Winjin' Pom was on the road again – but this time Ronnie was driving, his brother Reggie beside him. The Crows were speaking in loud voices, making sure that their prisoners could hear them.

'It's lovely up there on the clifftops, ain't it, Ron?'

'Yeah, Reggie – as long as you keep away from the edge.'

Reggie looked over his shoulder. In the back of the camper, Adelaide, Sydney, Frazer and Darwin were all lashed together back-to-back in an untidy parcel. Bruce the spider was caged inside a wire lettuce-strainer hung up on the wall.

'You're gonna get a lovely view of the white cliffs of Dover.'

'On your way down,' said Reggie. 'Hur, hur, hur!'

The Crows burst into song. 'There'll be Aussies over the white cliffs of Dover . . .'

Picking up speed, the Pom joined in the song. 'You think so? Just you wait and see!'

Faster and faster the Pom zoomed down the narrow lanes. It swayed from side to side, shaking up Crows and Aussies alike.

In the driving cab the Crows started to panic.

'Ease off, Ron,' said Reggie. 'We ain't in no hurry!'

'I can't ease off!' gasped Ronnie. 'I fink the pedal's broke!'

'Just don't panic! Let me take the wheel!'

'Righto!' said Ronnie. Lifting the steering wheel free, he passed it to his brother.

Reggie groaned. 'A word in your shell-like, Ronnie?'

'Yes, Reggie?'

'*Help!*' bellowed Reggie.

The Pom zoomed on, faster and faster and faster, heading straight for a narrow humpbacked bridge.

'Well,' muttered the Pom grimly. 'I suppose a van's gotta do what a van's gotta do . . .'

The Pom's big round eyes bulged and crossed with effort, and the front doors suddenly opened, not outwards but *upwards*, like stubby wings. The van shot on to the bridge, up and up and up . . .

The Winjin' Pom was flying!

Not like a bird, exactly – more like some early eccentric experimental flying-machine. It lumbered into the sky and wheeled clumsily round in a wobbly circle.

As the Pom banked and soared, high above the patchwork quilt of fields down below, Ronnie and Reggie, trapped in the suddenly door-less driving cab, hung on for their lives, clutching at the seats, the doorframes and each other.

In the back, the Aussies were too amazed to be afraid.

'We're flying,' murmured Darwin.

The roaring and wheezing of the Pom's engine suddenly cut out.

'We're gliding!' said Adelaide wonderingly.

Suddenly the Pom tilted forwards and began spinning towards the ground.

'We're crashing!' shrieked Sydney. The Aussies gave yells of alarm. Imprisoned in his lettuce-strainer, Bruce rattled about like a bean in a castanet . . .

Round and round, down and down, spun the Pom, in an apparently suicidal dive. Snatched free from the cab by centrifugal force, Ronnie and Reggie were thrown out of the gaping doors. Too scared to remember they were birds, they plummeted down and down. . . .

Just below, low buildings and tanks were grouped around what might have been a swimming-pool. It might have been, but it wasn't. The sign beside it read: 'E. PONG – SEWAGE FARM'.

Ronnie and Reggie plunged into the murky bubbling gunge . . .

The Pom chuckled wheezily. 'That's dropped them right in it!' Starting up its engine it pulled out of the spiral, swung round in a wide circle and swooped towards the ground. The door-wings slammed down and the Pom made a bumpy touch-down in a country lane. The shock of the landing jolted the lettuce-strainer from the wall, setting Bruce free. Adelaide managed to wriggle free of the coils of rope and untied the others.

'It's all right, we're down, Darwin,' she said.

'I'm just waiting for my stomach to catch up,' moaned Darwin.

Sydney was sitting bolt upright, eyes swivelling, going, 'Oooh! Oooh! Oooh!'

'Sydney?' said Adelaide. 'Sydney?'

'She's in shock,' said Frazer.

'Best place for her,' said Adelaide and went outside.

She ran round to the front of the Pom and patted its bumper.

'Top stuff, Pom! When did ya learn to fly?'

'About ten minutes ago,' groaned the Pom. 'I've had it. This is the end of the road.'

'No it ain't, Pom! A few litres of high octane, and she'll be apples, no worries!'

'Don't mock the afflicted,' pleaded the Pom. He made a feeble attempt to start his engine. It wheezed and clanked and died.

'Ah, that's nothing,' said Adelaide.

'It used to be an engine,' said the Pom bitterly.

'Don't worry about it,' said Adelaide. 'We've got to get to Studmare Hall.'

'OK,' said the Pom gloomily. 'Off you go.'

Frazer leaned out of the cab window. 'Aren't you gonna help us to restore the record to its rightful owner, Pom?'

'What for?'

Darwin popped his head out as well. 'So we can share the reward!' The Pom suddenly roared into life and trundled off down the lane. Adelaide ran after it, shouting, 'Come back you steaming great mong . . .'

★

Ron and Reggie plunged into the bubbling gunge . . .

PC Porker was driving the battered police car along the lanes, Sergeant Hog at his side, looking for the escaped prisoners.

They came to a crossroads. 'Where now, Sarge?' asked Porker.

'Comb the countryside, Porker. Comb the countryside!'

'Right, Sarge!' Producing a giant comb, Porker drove on.

The Pom drove through the wrought-iron gates of Studmare Hall, along the drive and up to the noble mansion itself. On the wall a notice read: STUDMARE HALL – ENGLISH HERITAGE – HIPPIES SHOT ON SIGHT.

The Aussies gathered outside the massive door, and Frazer heaved on the bell-pull. There was a rusty jangle, and it came away in his hand.

The doors opened and a mournful old foxhound in butler's uniform appeared. 'You rang?'

'No, it was the bell,' said Darwin.

The door slammed shut. Adelaide pounded until it opened again. The butler reappeared, carrying a blunderbuss. 'Go away! I won't tell you again!'

Bruce popped his head out of Frazer's pocket. 'Can I bite 'im?'

'We've brought back your Nellie Melba,' explained Sydney.

The butler bowed. 'I'll make up the spare room.'

'You don't understand, your Lordship,' squawked Sydney with an elaborate curtsy.

'My name is Jarvis,' said the old foxhound icily. 'I am her ladyship's butler. Her Ladyship is the only surviving daughter of the late Earl of . . .'

'Show him the record, Darwin,' said Adelaide. 'Before he uproots the whole family tree.'

Darwin opened the case and showed Jarvis the old record.

'Ah!' said Jarvis. 'Follow me!'

He led them through a long hall lined with family portraits and halted outside an elaborately decorated door. 'Wait here.'

He went through, closing the door behind him.

'Funny old feller,' said Frazer.

'She must be stinkin' rich,' said Adelaide. 'The size of the place!'

Sydney was ecstatic. 'Oh, this is where I belong!' She waved her fan. 'Look at all this culture!'

'You'd think they might have scraped it off,' muttered Darwin.

'Think of the upkeep,' said Adelaide.

'Think of the flamin' reward,' said Frazer.

The door opened and Jarvis said, 'Her Ladyship will see you.'

Inside an elaborately decorated salon, hung with glittering chandeliers, a very old horse lay dozing on a *chaise-longue*, her teeth in a crystal goblet at her side.

'Oh, your Ladyship!' breathed Sydney reverently.

There was a chorus of 'Hallos' and 'G'days' but the old mare dozed on. Jarvis gave her a respectful thump on the side of the head and she came to life and looked up at the Aussies.

'Do forgive me for not getting up!' she said, in an accent so amazingly posh they could hardly understand a word of it.

'What did she say?' whispered Sydney.

'I have no idea,' said Jarvis mournfully. 'I've scarcely understood a word she's said since 1938.'

Adelaide raised her voice. 'We've brought your record back, lady.'

'How frightfully good of you!'

'I think she's pleased,' said Sydney.

'We're from Oz,' explained Adelaide.

'Never mind, dear,' said her ladyship consolingly.

'Gullagaloona!' added Darwin.

'Bless you,' said Lady Studmare. She looked round the group. 'And now, you deserve a reward!'

Adelaide had picked out the key word. She gave Jarvis a nudge.

'Did she mention a reward?'

'She did.'

Lady Studmare took the record out of its case. 'I'm so grateful, I'm going to let you listen to it!'

'Oh, splendid!' said Sydney.

'Oh, *terrific!*' said the others.

'Oh, dear . . .' said Jarvis.

More by luck than judgement, the pursuing police had spotted the Pom, parked outside Studmare Hall. They zoomed up behind it. The strains of Dame Nellie Melba came floating out from the window. Sergeant Hog shuddered. 'There's murder being done in there!'

'Think they want a hand, Sarge?'

'Good thinking, Porker. That's a first for you.'

'Thanks, Sarge. Shall I call up the flying squad?'

Hog shook his head. 'They're at an acid house party.'

'That's criminal! Why weren't we invited?'

There was another piercing shriek from Dame Nellie. Hog drew his truncheon. 'Right, PC Porker – follow me!'

In the finest police tradition, Hog and Porker smashed down the front door, stampeded through the gallery, smashed down the second door into the salon and dashed in, truncheons waving. As they skidded to a halt by the *chaise-longue*, Sergeant Hog knocked over a stand which held a vase. The stand toppled sideways and crashed into the old fashioned gramophone, shattering the Melba record to fragments.

'Oh!' said Lady Studmare.

'Ooh!' screeched Sydney.

'Just a routine cock-up, Madam,' said Sergeant Hog.

The Pom was speeding away from Studmare Hall, the Aussies back in the front seat. Sydney was still very upset. 'They completely destroyed Nellie Melba!'

'I know,' said Darwin. 'We only heard about a minute of it!'

'There was another four minutes to go too,' said Sydney.

Adelaide chuckled. 'Aren't Pommy policemen wonderful!'

'Here, just a thought,' said the Pom. 'If music has charms to soothe the savage beast – why do lion tamers use a chair?'

Speeding happily along the winding lanes, the Pom raised a rusty voice. '*They call me Mimi* . . .'

A concerted shout came from inside the camper. 'Stop winjin', Pom!'

Chapter Seven

The Big Bang

Creaking and rattling along the country roads, producing the occasional rude noise from its exhaust pipe, the Winjin' Pom was headed for the seaside.

Adelaide and Sydney had the driving seat to themselves, Darwin and Frazer were dozing on the let-down bed in the back.

The Pom passed a road sign which said 'TO HASTINGS'.

'Ah, the Battle of Hastings,' said Sydney.

'1066!' said Adelaide.

'I know when it was, Adelaide.'

'The Poms lost.'

Bruce descended from the roof with his usual unnerving suddenness. 'Yeah, the Frogs creamed 'em!'

Determined to show off her superior historical knowledge, Sydney said, 'And King Harold turned to his men and said—'

'Frankly, my dear, I don't give a damn . . .' said a sleepy voice from the back. It was Darwin, deep in a *Gone With The Wind* dream. In the back of the camper, Frazer leaned over him. 'Dreamin' of Scarlett O'Hara again, Darwin?'

Darwin opened bleary eyes. 'Were you, Frazer? That's nice.' Shaking his head, Frazer tucked Darwin in with his teddy bear.

Suddenly the Pom swerved into a lay-by, gave a particularly loud and rude noise from its exhaust pipe and juddered to a halt. 'I should never have had that curry,' he belched.

In his art-deco penthouse office, Jay Gee Chicago crouched over his Mighty Wurlitzer, belting out the strains of 'New York, New York'. As the last rumbling notes died away, a withered claw reached out and jabbed a button marked 'Howard'.

A buzzer buzzed, and Howard hurried nervously forward. 'Something I can get you, Jay Gee?'

Jay Gee stared malevolently at his perspiring assistant, reflected in the driving mirror fitted to the Wurlitzer.

'Don't sweat, Howard,' he croaked softly. 'I don't like it when you sweat.'

Howard laughed nervously. 'I guess I shouldn't be so highly strung.'

'Yes you should, Howard – wid pianna wire!' Jay Gee swung round to face him. 'You hired the Crows – and they failed, Howard! A bunch of Australian tourists ran rings round 'em. I want 'em taken care of.'

'Sure thing, Jay Gee. I'll book 'em in at the Hilton!' Jay Gee's cane cracked down on Howard's head. 'I mean the Crows, nut head. I want 'em dead – and this time, permanently.'

'Right, Jay Gee, I'll ring Joe Armadillo . . .'

As Howard reached for the phone, the cane cracked him across the knuckles. 'No, Howard. *You* hired, *you* fire – bang! Or better still – boom!'

In the Crows' office on Nelson's Column, Ronnie Crow was laboriously building a house of cards. The lift doors swished open and Reggie entered. He strode across the office and slapped Ronnie on the back. 'Any messages?' Ronnie jumped and the house of cards collapsed. 'No, no messages, Reggie. Oh, Jay Gee rang.'

Reggie grabbed Ronnie by the lapels. 'Jay Gee! What did he want? What did you tell him?'

'I boxed clever, Reggie.'

'Thank 'eavens for that! What did you say?'

'I said we failed.'

Reggie clipped him one across the bonce. 'Ronnie, Ronnie!' He clouted him again. 'Are you in there, Ronnie?' Another clout. 'Hallo? The lights are on but there's no one home!'

'I must be there, Reggie, I can hear someone knocking.'

'Ronnie, watch my beak. Did you tell Jay Gee about the camper?'

'Nah! Er, what camper?'

'The one that flies, Ronnie! The one that talks!' Reggie put his hand on his heart for emphasis. *'The one we got to have!'*

Jay Gee's stretch limo got Howard to the airport, and Jay Gee's amazing wealth got him a seat on Concorde. As night fell in Trafalgar Square, Howard was lurking in the Crows' underground car-park. He wore the standard gangster outfit of black overcoat and black trilby and he carried the usual violin case. Howard was thrilled with his deadly mission. The voice-over from a thousand B-movies was playing inside his head. *'I made it to the basement underneath Nelson's Column by nine. The Crows' garage was deserted. There was a faint smell of pigeons – dead pigeons . . . Or were they? I reached the Crows' private elevator and slipped inside . . . '* As the lift doors opened, Howard tripped and disappeared inside the lift with a crash and a yell.

Upstairs in the lavish, marble-walled bathroom of the penthouse, Ronnie and Reggie, immaculate in evening dress, were adjusting their black bow ties before a mirror.

'Oh, it's in a very good cause, Ron,' Reggie was saying.

'I like a good cause, Reggie.'

'We should raise loads of dosh for this one.'

'Er, what cause is it, exactly, Reggie?'

'It's for charity, Reggie. The Crow brothers' gymnasium for underprivileged starlings.'

'I didn't know we was building one of them.'

'That's 'cos we ain't, Ronnie . . .'

In the lift Howard had produced a book called *How to Blow Up Anything* and was flicking through it feverishly, steam coming out of his ears. *'I had to work fast. Lemme see, bridges, boats . . . elevators . . . It all seemed pretty straightforward.'* Turning to the right page, Howard found himself looking at a complicated circuit diagram. For a moment his eyes crossed in horror. Then, mastering his panic, he took tools and explosives from his violin case and removed the lift's control panel. With trembling fingers, he set to work . . .

A frantic few minutes later, Howard replaced the panel, and stepped back. 'That's it! Once the down button is pressed – Crow Casserole! Yummy!'

Up in the penthouse, Ronnie pressed the call button. The lift doors closed and it started to rise – with Howard still inside.

Reggie and Ronnie stood waiting for the lift.

'A flying camper,' said Reggie. 'Reggie see, Reggie wants!'

'Don't worry,' Ronnie tapped his beak. 'I've got every starling in London out looking for it.'

The lift doors slid open, revealing a quivering Howard.

The Crows were delighted to see their mate from the States.

'Howard!' said Reggie. 'What a pleasant surprise!'

Howard tried to leap from the lift. The Crow brothers shoved him back in. 'Where yer going, Howard?' asked Ronnie interestedly.

'Anywhere!' whimpered Howard. 'You go on, I'll wait here . . .'

Reggie followed him in. 'No, I insist – you're coming with us. You'll have a great night out, Howard.'

'Yeah, pull a few birds, eh?' said Ronnie.

'Make your evening go with a bang!' said Reggie.

'Lemme out!' screamed Howard. 'I'm claustrophobic!'

'Yeah?' said Ronnie, entering the lift. 'I'm Capricorn. My stars said I'd be all over the place today.' He reached for the 'down' button.

'Don't press that button!' screamed Howard.

'That's right,' said Ronnie, surprised. 'They said that too.'

He pressed the button, there was a shattering explosion, and the lift doors vanished in a cloud of smoke.

After a moment, Reggie's voice came out of the smoke.

'Howard?' it said gently. 'Could we have a word?'

The Winjin' Pom trundled on towards Hastings, Adelaide at the wheel, Frazer and Darwin beside her. Darwin was buried in an old film magazine. Sydney's head popped through the back curtain, adorned with an old black beret she'd found in the cupboard. She twisted the rear-view mirror to study the effect. 'Mother always said I looked like Ingrid Bergman,' she remarked.

Adelaide straightened the mirror. 'Sure she didn't mean Humphrey Bogart?'

'Now that's not fair, Addy,' protested Darwin. 'Bogart was much shorter. Interestingly enough, he never had to wear built-up shoes. Mind you, he might have had a built-up hat, but I've never seen any reports of built-up shoes at all . . .'

As Darwin rambled on, Bruce dropped down from the ceiling. 'Why's Darwin always chewin' on about old movies, Frazer?' he asked.

'Old Darwin's fair dinkum, Brucie,' said Frazer tolerantly. 'Life just bowled him a bad ball.'

'You mean he's daft?'

'No, Bruce. Darwin just had a deprived childhood – deprived of cricket, mainly.'

'Some wombats have all the luck!' Bruce giggled. 'Hey, Fraze, what did one fly say to the other?'

'I dunno, Brucie. What did one fly say to the other?'

'Your man's undone!' With another manic giggle, Bruce zoomed upwards.

The Pom rattled peacefully on. Things were going pretty smoothly, thought Adelaide. She should have known they were heading for trouble.

It was waiting just ahead in the massive shapes of Aberdeen Angus and Big Willie Galloway – two motor-biking bulls. They were a fearsome sight. They wore black leather jackets with THE RAGING BULLS on the back, jeans and swastika-decorated motorcycle boots. Angus wore a T-shirt with 'OCH AYE THE MOO' on it, and a green tartan waistcoat. Willie had a green-striped T-shirt and a ring through his punched-up nose. Both had vicious-looking curved horns. They were two *bad* bulls.

Feet up on their handlebars, Big Willie and Angus were relaxing with a few cans of lager in a lay-by when the Pom trundled by. Unfortunately, the Pom chose that moment to emit a particularly rude noise, accompanied by a cloud of black smoke, from its exhaust pipe. Coughing in the oily black fumes, the two biker bulls snorted in indignation, kicked their bikes into life, and set off in pursuit.

Unaware of the approaching danger, Adelaide was driving peacefully along when two big bikes bearing two big bulls revved up alongside.

'Hey, Wullie!' roared Angus, riding up next to the camper.

'Take a look at this!'

'D'ye ken what it is, Angus?'

'Ay, Wullie – it's a mobile bedpan!'

The bulls roared with laughter.

Willie leered across at Adelaide. 'Hey, you! Have ye a licence for this thunderbox?'

The Pom's eyes bulged in indignation.

'Ignore 'em,' whispered Adelaide to the other Aussies.

Darwin stared in amazement at the two outlandish figures on the motor bikes. 'Who are they?'

'Foreigners!' said Sydney scathingly.

'They call me Aberdeen Angus,' growled the nearer bull.

'Ay, and I'm Big Willie Galloway,' roared the other.

Angus glared threateningly at Darwin. 'You're no verra friendly are ye – ye stuck-up wee pillock!'

He turned to his fellow biker, 'Hey, Willie! Let's gie it a wee bittie push!'

The motor bikes dropped back behind the Pom.

The Aussies looked apprehensively at each other, wondering what was coming next. They soon found out.

Riding parallel behind the Pom, the two massive bikes increased speed and delivered simultaneous bashes to the camper's rear bumper.

'Ouch!' grunted the Pom.

In the cab the Aussies were thrown forward by the impact. They yelled in alarm.

'Can I bite 'em?' squeaked Bruce.

There was another jolt, then another. Then, waving and jeering, the biker bulls roared past the camper and disappeared into the distance.

Darwin sighed with relief. 'Lager louts!'

'Just looking for trouble!' said Sydney.

'Good!' growled the Pom, eyes bulging with anger. ''Cos that's just what I'm going to give 'em!'

'No, Pom! No!' yelled Adelaide, but it was already too late.

'Mobile bedpan!' snorted the Pom indignantly, and surged forward like a Formula One racer.

Adelaide wrestled with the wheel as the countryside flashed by. 'Strewth, we're doing ninety!' she exclaimed.

'Mother!' screamed Sydney, sticking her head in her fire-bucket.

'What would Jimmy Cagney say at a time like this?' wondered Darwin.

With one voice the others answered him. '*Help!*'

Zooming along well above the speed limit, the astonished bikers heard something roaring up behind them.

The vengeful Pom bore down grimly . . . Seconds later, bikes and bikers were flying through the air. They landed in a tangled heap at the side of the road, as the Pom roared triumphantly past. The reeling bulls staggered to their feet – and head-butted each other out of sheer frustration . . .

'But I like you fellas,' pleaded Howard.

He was with the Crows on their penthouse terrace, on top of Nelson's Column, high above Trafalgar Square.

Reggie and Ronnie, cleaned up, bandages gone, back in their snappy dark suits, were sitting happily at twin tables sipping exotic cocktails – the kind with paper umbrellas in.

Howard, however, was far from happy. Stripped of his gangster coat and hat, shivering in natty plaid slacks and Hawaiian shirt, he was perched on the end of a short plank, jutting out from the low wall round the terrace, a sheer drop below him.

'Honest, fellas,' sobbed Howard. 'I *like* you!'

Reggie sipped his cocktail. 'Hear that, Ronnie – he likes us.'

'Everybody likes us, Ronnie – eventually.'

'Gimme a break, boys,' pleaded Howard. 'I got vertigo!'

'I wouldn't call it far to go,' said Reggie.

'No,' said Ronnie. 'Only about an 'undred and fifty feet.'
The Crow brothers were famous for their sense of humour.

'You been a naughty boy, Howard,' said Reggie sadly.
He jumped on the other end of the plank and Howard shot
off into thin air. Somehow he grabbed the plank on his way
down. 'Listen, fellas . . .'

'Ain't you gone yet, Howard?' asked Reggie mildly, and
spanged the plank again.

Desperately Howard hung on. 'It was all Jay Gee's idea.
Rubbing me out won't stop him – he never gives up!'

Reggie bounced the board again and Howard shot up in
the air.

Once again he grabbed the end of the board on his way
down. 'You gotta get him first, see! And I'm the only one
knows how!'

The Crows looked thoughtfully at each other.

'You could take over his entire operation!' screamed
Howard desperately.

They hauled him in off the plank and gave him a cocktail.

'All his business secrets are in here,' said Howard tapping
his own head. 'I've got everything you need. The contacts,
the know-how, the total lack of scruples!'

The terrace phone rang and Ronnie picked it up. 'Yeah?
Hastings Road? Got it.' He turned to Reggie. 'The flying
camper's 'eading for 'astings.'

Howard's ears twitched. 'A flying camper, fellas?'

Ronnie looked at his brother. 'Shall we tell him, Reggie?'

'Speak to me,' begged Howard. 'Did you say a flying
camper?'

'Can we trust you, Howard?' asked Reggie.

Howard looked hurt. 'Reggie, baby, need you ask?'

Reggie lowered his voice. 'This camper really really flies.'

'Yeah,' said Ronnie. '*And* talks . . .'

'The camper talks, Jay Gee,' whispered Howard. 'And
flies.' He had finally managed to slip away from the Crows.
Naturally he'd headed straight for the nearest phone box
to betray them to Jay Gee. The betrayal wasn't going too
well.

In his office, Jay Gee Chicago stared unbelievingly at the

phone. 'Congratulations, Howard,' he rasped. 'I see you finally made the rubber room.'

Howard looked cautiously around. 'I've convinced them I'm working against you, Jay Gee.'

'Yeah? You convinced me too!'

'I'll bring you the camper, Jay Gee! I'll fly back, OK?'

'Sure, Howard, sure,' said Jay Gee's voice soothingly.

'All right, Jay Gee. I'd better go before the Crows get wise . . .'

In his office, Jay Gee put down the phone. 'Get wise – *any* of those guys? Huh, I should live so long!'

Still, he thought, a talking, flying camper. Suppose it was all true . . ?

Chapter Eight

Bulls in a China Shop

The Pom drove through the quiet country lanes into a quaint old English village and parked outside a quaint old English tourist trap – YE OLDE BONE CHINA GIFT SHOPPE. The Aussies piled out of the camper and went inside. It was a refined sort of place, its shelves and stands packed with an assortment of dainty-looking cups, plates, jugs and bowls, some obviously antique.

'What are we doing here, Sydney?' asked Adelaide.

'Mother wants a nice bit of Spode.'

'Well, I wouldn't buy it here,' said Adelaide, eyeing the antiques. 'Some of this stuff's second-hand.'

An elderly female hedgehog appeared from the back of the shop. 'It's ten per cent off everything, dear – unless you're Americans,' she said, in a voice as dainty as her china.

'We're from Gullagaloona,' said Sydney.

'In Australia,' added Adelaide.

'Oh, my niece works in Melbourne. Do you know the Pink Pussy Massage parlour? I'm Mrs Diddle, by the way. Are you looking for anything special, dear?'

'Spode,' said Sydney, in a 'nothing-but-the-best' voice.

'What about a nice antique teapot?' Mrs Diddle held up a teapot, or rather the remains of one. 'Only two hundred and fifty pounds.'

'Where's the spout?' asked Sydney. 'And the lid – and the handle?'

'I could knock a bit off, dear.'

'If you knocked any more off you wouldn't have a teapot,' said Adelaide.

'How much did you want to spend, dear?' asked Mrs

Diddle. 'I've got lots more junk in the stockroom – oops – I mean, stock, in the junk room.'

There was a sudden roar of engines from outside. It got louder and louder, and then stopped.

Frazer peered outside. 'It's those Raging Bulls!'

The Aussies headed for the door, but it was already too late. The door was flung open, revealing the massive forms of Aberdeen Angus and Big Willie Galloway.

'Do ma eyes deceive me, Angus?' said Willie happily.

Angus grinned evilly. 'Och, it's so nice tae bump into auld acquaintances again – and gie 'em an Aberdeen handshake!' He aimed a sudden head-butt at Darwin, who ducked and fell over backwards.

Roaring angrily, the Raging Bulls chased the Aussies around the shop. With the carelessness of bulls in a china shop – which is just what they were, of course – they snatched up pieces of valuable china and sent them flying through the air. Mrs Diddle fielded each and every one with the expertise of a world cup goalkeeper, catching the last one on the end of her pointed nose.

Not a single piece was broken, as the Aussies disappeared out of the door, with the Raging Bulls in hot pursuit.

Mrs Diddle stood in the doorway, waving her fist. 'Out, you cheeky monkeys – and don't come back, or I'll have your horns for hatstands!'

She turned away, slamming the door. Unfortunately, she slammed it so hard that every shelf and stand in the place collapsed. The air filled with the sound of breaking china, and poor Mrs Diddle was left standing amongst the shattered remains of her stock. 'Me Ming!' she sobbed. 'Oh, me Ming!'

Outside the shop, the Aussies dived into the back of the van. Unfortunately, the raging Bulls dived in after them.

The van rocked to and fro and sounds of general mayhem came from inside.

Big Willie and Angus emerged with the air of a job well done.

'That was no' bad,' said Willie.

'Ay, no' bad at all,' agreed Angus.

They climbed on their motor bikes and roared away.

Inside the smashed-up camper everything was quiet. Then Darwin appeared, head draped with the remains of a shattered deck chair. Adelaide bobbed up beside him. She was hopping mad. 'Right – that does it! Sydney?'

Sydney popped up too, her fire-bucket over her head.

Adelaide went on with her roll-call. 'Frazer!'

Frazer appeared, a banana skin on his head.

Adelaide looked round. 'Where's Brucie?'

Bruce dropped down from the ceiling. 'I would've bit 'em – only there wasn't time.'

Sydney took her head out of her bucket. 'What a mess!' she moaned.

'And who got us into it?' whispered Adelaide. 'That two-toned trouble-maker – the Pom! What's more, I reckon he'd do it again.'

'He would too,' agreed Sydney.

'And do you know why?' continued Adelaide. 'Because he's a Pom!'

'Middle stump, Adelaide,' said Frazer.

'I'm not normally racist,' went on Adelaide. 'Except about Poms.'

Frazer nodded. 'They've got a completely different mentality.'

'You can't trust 'em,' said Sydney.

Sadly the Aussies agreed that Poms were lazy, dishonest, dirty, ate smelly food and had dubious morals.

'I wouldn't want one for a neighbour,' admitted Darwin.

'You couldn't move for them in Guildford,' complained Sydney.

'And they all stick together,' said Adelaide. 'Let's go outside.' They climbed out of the van and moved a little way away.

''Ere, where are you lot going?' asked the Pom suspiciously. 'Oh, don't tell me, I'm only the blooming transport.'

Once they were safely out of earshot, Adelaide revealed her plan. 'We've got to get rid of him!'

Sydney was shocked. 'Get rid of him? But that's . . .'

'Murder!' whispered Darwin.

'Don't be daft,' said Adelaide. 'We'll just give him the Big E.'

Darwin patted his pockets. 'Don't think I've got one . . .'

'Look at the strife he's caused us,' urged Adelaide. 'The cops, the Crows, the Bulls . . . And whoever heard of a camper deciding where it's going to take you. It's just not on – he's got to go!'

'How'll we get around without him?' asked Darwin practically.

'Oh for cripes sake, Darwin! We're the Gullagaloona Backpackers, ain't we?' She gave the club rallying cry. 'Where are we from?'

'Gullagaloona!'

'What do we want?'

'To see the world!'

'How'll we see it?'

'Leg it about!' chanted the Aussies. 'Gullagaloona!'

'Or,' said Adelaide thoughtfully, 'we could get another camper.'

A short time later they were drawing up outside DODGY AUTOS LTD, a rather seedy-looking used-car dealer. It consisted of a battered caravan surrounded by an assortment of even more dilapidated vehicles. It was run, as it happened, by a sharply dressed ferret called Des Devious, a distant cousin of Sid Shifty.

Des was on his mobile phone. 'I'm sorry, squire, you'd better read your warranty. It covers absolutely everything *except* parts and labour. So there's no engine – what do you expect for two and a half grand? Pleasure doing business with you!' He put down the phone and turned to the Aussies. 'And what can I do you for?'

'G'day,' said Adelaide. 'We're looking for a camper.'

Des beamed. 'Tell you what, squires and squiresses – is this your lucky day – or is this your lucky day!' He raised his voice.

'Arnold! You know that turbo super camper travelette de luxe? Push it round to the front.' He turned back to the Aussies. 'You wanna camper, I gotta camper!'

Darwin moved closer to him and said firmly, 'We don't want one that flies.'

Des backed away. 'No, well, you wouldn't, would you?'

'Or gets us into fights.'

'No, who would?'

'Yours doesn't talk, does it?'

'It's kept *schtum* up to now.'

'Good. Just wanted to make it quite clear what we're looking for.'

'Mustn't fly, fight or rabbit,' said Des. He looked worriedly at the others, nodding towards Darwin. 'Is he all right?'

'We were hoping you might do a part exchange,' said Sydney.

'He needs a bit of attention,' said Adelaide.

'Oh well, we all do,' said Des.

'But basically, he's quite reliable,' said Frazer.

'Of course,' said Adelaide, 'you could always cannibalize him for spare parts.'

Des, who thought they were still talking about Darwin, looked at her in horror.

'Take a look,' said Sydney, pointing towards the Pom.

'Oh, that's him,' said Des with relief.

'Well?' asked Adelaide. 'How much?'

Des studied the Pom. 'Fifty quid.'

'Fifty?' Adelaide was delighted. They'd only paid twenty.

'Yeah, you gimme fifty quid and I'll take it off your hands.'

Sydney was shocked. '*We* pay *you*?'

'I'm doing you a favour, lady. That thing's about as much use as a concrete parachute.'

A young hedgehog in greasy overalls drove a camper van round to the front. It was almost as old and battered as the Pom and it had just been painted bright pink. 'Now that,' said Des proudly, 'is what you *can* call a camper.'

Before very long the deal was done. Des reluctantly gave them a tenner on the Pom, and the Aussies gathered round to say goodbye.

Strangely enough, they were feeling a bit sad.

'No hard feelings, eh, Pom?' said Adelaide.

'Nothing personal,' said Sydney.

'Just time for the new ball,' said Frazer.

'I worked my rings off for you,' said the Pom bitterly.

'Oh, don't perform,' said Adelaide, suddenly losing patience. 'You've been a pain in the pouch since we met ya!'

Tears flowed from the Pom's windscreen-wipers. 'Go on, kick a van when he's down. Throw me aside like an old log book! Why don't you rip off me plates and have done with it?'

'Come on, let's go,' said Adelaide gruffly.

Turning their backs on the Pom, the Aussies moved towards their brightly coloured new van.

Darwin was still unhappy as Adelaide drove their new vehicle towards Beachy Head.

'Wonder what'll happen to him?' he mused.

'Give it a break, Darwin,' said Adelaide, who was feeling a bit guilty herself.

'Poor old Pom,' sighed Darwin. 'He wasn't so bad.'

'Darwin,' said Adelaide, beckoning him towards her.

Darwin leaned forward obligingly. 'Yes, Addie?'

Adelaide delivered a sharp clip over the ear.

'Ouch!' said Darwin, and shut up.

Not far behind them the Crows were zooming along in their newly repaired limousine.

'Boys, not so fast,' protested Howard.

'Shut it, Howard,' said Reggie politely.

The sinister black car sped on.

The Aussies parked their new van on the clifftop, and stretched out on the cliff-edge, gazing out to sea.

The misty blueness made Sydney feel romantic. 'Did I ever tell you about the time I danced *Giselle* in Yacamunda?'

'Frequently.'

'I could've had a wonderful career.'

Adelaide leaned towards Darwin. 'She completely blew the audition for *Swan Lake*.

'Why was that, Adelaide?' asked Frazer.

'Because she's an ostrich, ya dill!'

Darwin was sound asleep, dreaming he was Jimmy

Cagney in *White Heat*. 'Top of the world, Ma,' he muttered. 'Top of the world!'

Just behind them, a black limousine coasted quietly to a halt. Howard and the Crows got out.

'It's them!' whispered Reggie.

Howard waved. 'Hi guys—' He shut up as Reggie's hand clamped down on his muzzle.

'Let's get 'em,' said Ronnie.

With Howard between them, the Crows advanced.

'Guess who?' said Reggie.

The Aussies whipped round. 'It's the Crows!'

'And I'm Howard, their friend,' simpered Howard. The Crows looked at him. 'Well, almost.'

'What do you want?' quavered Sydney.

Reggie pointed to the pink camper. 'Need you ask?'

'But that's not the Pom,' protested Darwin.

'Think I'm stupid?' jeered Reggie.

'One question at a time,' said Adelaide.

'You've painted it, 'aven't you?' accused Ronnie.

'We sold it!' said Sydney.

Ronnie didn't believe her. 'You sold a flying camper? What's worth millions?' He laughed mockingly. 'Think we just fell out of the nest?'

'Come on, Howard,' said Reggie. 'We'll fly it out to sea.'

'To see what, Reggie?' asked Ronnie.

'You are a wag, Ron,' said Reggie patiently.

Ignoring the Aussies, they urged Howard towards the pink camper. Darwin called after them. 'But that's not—'

'Darwin!' said Adelaide quietly. 'Let 'em find out, eh?'

Howard didn't want to go. 'Not me, boys, I'm strictly an observer.'

Reggie wouldn't listen. 'You're coming, Howard!'

'But I hate planes!'

'This is a camper,' said Ronnie, shoving him inside.

Far below, on a strip of sand at the bottom of the cliffs, the Raging Bulls were sitting on their motor bikes, eating ice-creams and gazing at the sea.

'I'm bored, Wullie,' complained Angus. 'There's nothing tae vandalize here.'

Willie's only reply was to give him a friendly kick.

'Hey, you. Watch it,' growled Angus.

They started to brawl and squabble, unaware of the fate hanging over them.

The Crows were sitting in the front seat of the pink camper, a quivering Howard between them. Ronnie was at the wheel.

'Come on, my old son, show us what you can do,' urged Reggie.

Ronnie looked at Howard. 'OK, Howard?'

Howard sobbed and covered his face with his hands.

'Chocks away! Let's go!' yelled Reggie.

The pink camper zoomed towards the cliffs. It shot straight over the edge and out into midair – and dropped like a stone towards the beach.

'It'll soar like a bird in a minute,' said Reggie confidently. But it didn't.

Down, down, down went the camper . . . heading straight for the Raging Bulls who looked up in amazement at the pink shape dropping towards them.

A row of Aussie heads peered over the clifftop – just in time to see the pink camper land on the Bulls and smash itself to pieces. Adelaide looked at the others. 'Whoever heard of a flying camper anyway?'

As the sound of the crash died away there was a moment of silence.

Howard, a born survivor, clawed his way out of the wreckage.

Seconds later the Crow brothers emerged as well.

'Er, Reggie?'

'Yes, Ronnie?'

'I think we could work on the landing.'

'No camper,' said Sydney. 'What are we going to do?'

They heard a familiar engine-noise, and the poop-poop of a horn.

'It's the Pom!' yelled Darwin.

The Pom moved steadily towards them along the cliffs. It came level – and drove straight past without stopping.

They ran after it shouting. 'Come back, Pom! We're sorry! Come back!'

The Pom chuckled quietly to itself. 'And the moral of that is – a friend in need is a pain in the clutch!'

Whistling happily the Pom trundled on its way – but not very fast . . .

Chapter Nine

Haunted

The rain had been pouring down steadily for days. The fields were soggy, the roads were soggy and as night fell, the Winjin' Pom, parked in a lay-by, was soggiest of all. 'Look at it! Wanna know how wet it is? I've seen fish drown.'

Inside the camper, things weren't all that much better. The place had been tidied up a bit, there were pans and buckets set out to catch the numerous drips, and on the central table the Aussies were playing Monopoly.

Darwin moved his little top hat along the board, and landed on Bruce's territory. The little schoolboy spider was crouching behind a rampart of hotels, a pile of money beside him. 'OK, Darwin – that's another seven hundred and fifty dollars.'

Darwin waved the last of his capital – two one-dollar bills. 'Oh dear – I don't think I've got that much.'

'You'll have to sell something, Darwin,' advised Frazer.

'I've got nothing to sell.'

'Then sell that, dill-brain!' said Bruce, blowing a vicious raspberry.

Darwin looked hurt and Adelaide said protectively, 'I'll lend you the money, Darwin.'

'Thanks, Addie.'

'That ain't fair,' squeaked Bruce.

'*Isn't* fair, Brucie,' corrected Frazer.

'See?' said Bruce. 'Frazer says it ain't fair as well.'

'If I want to help Darwin,' began Adelaide.

'For heaven's sake,' sighed Sydney, 'why go on? It's obvious Bruce has won.'

'Not while I've still got houses on Piccadilly.'

'Brucie's got hotels on everything,' said Darwin gloomily.

'Yeah – by sneakin' 'em on when we weren't looking!'

Bruce glared at her from behind his hotel barricades. 'Are you saying I'm cheating, Addie?'

'I'm saying the players shouldn't be allowed on the board.'

'Oh, let's pack it in, Addie,' said Darwin wearily.

'Why the blazes should I?'

'Because I'm top of the wozza!' crowed Bruce.

'Come here, you evil-minded mongrel,' yelled Adelaide, making a grab for him.

'No, Addie,' protested Darwin. He tried to stop her, and sent the Monopoly board flying.

'I'll bite yer, I'll bite yer!' squeaked Bruce.

'Adelaide, please, show some restraint,' begged Sydney.

'Missed me! Missed me!' taunted Bruce.

'Five days of rain,' said Adelaide tragically. 'No wonder we're all a bit snakey.'

'I'd give anything for a bed in a nice warm hotel,' said Darwin.

'It'll cost you another seven hundred and fifty,' said Bruce.

'Oh, shut up, you marshmallow!' snapped Darwin. Everyone looked at him in amazement. There was a flash of lightning and the rain came down harder than ever.

'*I'm winjin' in the rain,*' sang the Pom.
'*I'm winjin' in the rain,*
I've a miserable feeling
I'm leaking again . . .'

Outside, the Crow brothers' long black car was nosing its way through the downpour.

Reggie stared through the windscreen at the driving rain. 'We'll never find 'em in this, Ronnie.'

'It's the only car we've got, Reggie,' said his brother.

Inside the Pom, Adelaide had started to iron her spare dungarees. Frazer was reading a cricketing magazine, and Sydney was buried in *Great British Ghosts*.

On the bed, Darwin was dreaming he was somewhere over the rainbow. 'Tap your heels together three times,' he murmured. 'And think to yourself, "There's no place like home . . ." '

Bruce dropped down and dangled in front of Frazer's magazine.

'Hey, Fraze.'

'Yes, Brucie?'

'I done me first web!' murmured Bruce shyly.

Frazer looked up at the untidy little knot of threads.

'Er . . . first rate, Brucie. First rate,' he murmured tactfully.

Adelaide looked up from her ironing and glanced at Sydney's book.

'What a load of Pommy ponk!'

Darwin opened his eyes. 'What is?'

'Ghosts! The old white-sheet walkabout.'

'I wouldn't expect you to believe in them,' said Sydney. 'Ghosts are an earthly manifestation of a spiritual presence. There's nothing to be frightened of.'

Bruce yo-yo'd down from the ceiling, wrapped in a white handkerchief. 'Wooo! Wooo!' he wailed.

Sydney squawked and ducked into her fire-bucket. The ghost blew a raspberry and shot upwards again.

'He gets over-excited,' said Frazer tolerantly.

Adelaide tapped her head with the iron to test the heat. 'He gets over-everything.'

Suddenly Darwin sat bolt upright on the bed. 'Addie,' he quavered. 'We're moving!'

Adelaide dived through the curtain to the driving seat. 'OK, Pom, knock it off!'

'It ain't me,' grumbled the Pom. 'I ain't doing it.'

'Yer handbrake must have slipped.'

'Then why am I rolling *up*hill?'

Adelaide stared through the windscreen in alarm.

'Strewth!' she murmured.

The Pom was right – they were rolling uphill.

A black car flashed by going the other way.

Ronnie turned to his brother. 'It was them! It was them!'

'Why didn't you stop?' snarled Reggie.

Ronnie considered. 'I dunno. Er, ask me one on sport . . .'

Through the windscreen of the Pom the terrified Aussies found themselves staring out at a dark, gloomy-looking, turreted Gothic mansion illuminated by lightning flashes and surrounded by twisted, withered trees. It looked like Dracula's castle on a bad day. Drawn by some uncanny force, the Pom drove up the drive, and parked by the front door.

There was a wooden sign-board hanging crookedly from a post: 'PHILTHY PLACE – VACANCIES.'

'It's a hotel!' gasped Darwin. 'A real bed. Hot water.'

'It looks a bit . . . well, a bit . . .' said Frazer dubiously.

'I think I'd rather stay here,' said Sydney.

Adelaide produced an umbrella from her pouch. 'Suit yourself, Sydney – but you'll be on your own.'

'In that case,' Sydney tapped Darwin on the shoulder, 'are you coming or not?'

Huddling under Adelaide's umbrella, the Aussies hurried for the shelter of the porch, a big stone arch with gargoyles on either side. The one on the right had its tongue lolling out.

Adelaide banged on the heavy oak door. The door creaked open. The Aussies hurried inside.

'Looks nice out,' rumbled the right-hand gargoyle, as they disappeared inside.

'Yeah,' agreed the other. 'I'll get mine out.' It protruded an amazingly long tongue to match the first's.

The Aussies found themselves in the dimly lit foyer of what had once been a luxury hotel. Cobwebs hung from the crystal chandeliers, and the reception desk was thick with dust.

'Hallo,' called Adelaide.

'*Allo, allo, allo . . .* ' replied the echoes.

'Anybody about?'

'*Out, out, out . . .*'

'They're Poms, Sydney,' said Adelaide. 'Probably hiding in the cellar hoping we'll all choof off.'

'*Choof off, choof off, chooof off . . .*' said the echoes.

'It said vacancies!' protested Darwin.

Adelaide sniffed. 'It said welcome to Britain at the airport.'

Sydney saw a bell push on the counter, and a notice

which read, 'Please Ring for Attention'. She thumped the bell, producing a deep tolling note that shook the old house.

'Strewth!' said Adelaide. 'That was loud enough to wake the dead.'

'*Dead, dead, dead* . . .' boomed the echoes.

'I hope it doesn't,' quavered Darwin.

'You're such a wimp, Darwin,' muttered Adelaide.

Sydney was studying the register. 'Look!' she squawked. 'We're already booked in!'

Scrawled across the page were the words 'Gullagaloona Backpackers.'

The Aussies gasped – all except Adelaide.

'Maybe the place is haunted,' said Darwin nervously.

'Maybe it's "Let's-wind-up-Adelaide" night,' growled the wallaby. She raised her voice. 'I want to speak to the manager!'

Everything went black. All you could see were the Aussies' fearful eyes glowing in the darkness.

'OK, who did that?' demanded Adelaide.

No reply.

Another pair of eyes descended from the ceiling and a voice piped, 'What do you call an organized nun?'

'Put the lights on, Bruce!'

'Sister-matic!' giggled Bruce.

'The *lights*, Bruce.'

'Wasn't me,' said Bruce sulkily.

'Could be the storm,' said Darwin.

'Or a power cut,' suggested Sydney.

Once again, Adelaide's pouch came to the rescue. She produced candles, one for each of them, struck a match and lit them. As the little flames flickered against their faces a jeering voice came from above. 'Happy birthday to you – happy birthday to you – happy birthday, dear Addie . . .'

Adelaide looked up. 'Want to become an endangered species, Bruce?'

A raspberry floated down from the darkness overhead.

Darwin's candle went out. Adelaide struck another match to relight it. Before the match reached it, Darwin's candle relit of its own accord. Then the match blew out.

Adelaide glared upwards, shaking her fist. 'I'll get ya, ya hairy little horror!'

'I tell ya, it ain't me,' piped Bruce.

'OK, Darwin,' said Adelaide briskly. 'You check upstairs.'

'U-u-upstairs?'

'Off you go, Darwin.'

'But what if the floor opens up like in *Poltergeist* and becomes a bottomless chasm and I'm dragged down by a horde of gibbering fiends?'

'Then we'll know it's not safe to go upstairs, won't we, Darwin?'

'Let's go back to the Pom,' pleaded Sydney. 'This place is obviously deserted.'

'It's an English guest house,' snapped Adelaide. 'They're all like this!'

Outside, the Pom muttered, 'If anyone's wondering how I am, I'm cold, wet, tired and fed up to the back bumper, thanks for asking!'

A black car appeared quietly out of the darkness. 'It's the camper,' said Ronnie.

'Thanks, Ron,' said Reggie.

'Stone the crows!' muttered the Pom, and disappeared hastily round the corner of the house.

Darwin crept nervously up the stairs. He was nearly half-way up when his candle left his hand and floated ahead, as if carried by some invisible form. Darwin yelled and tumbled backwards.

Adelaide picked him up at the bottom of the stairs.

'My candle! It floated upstairs by itself!' he shrieked.

'Oh, Darwin, don't be such a dill.'

A ghastly howl rang through the foyer. Even Bruce was scared and dropped down to join his fellow Aussies. 'Who did that?' he squeaked.

Sydney stuck her head in her bucket – and withdrew it with a yell when a huge white flower sprouted from the sand – and shot water in her eye.

'Pull yourself together,' said Adelaide. 'It's only the plumbing.'

A secret panel suddenly opened in the wall and Frazer, who was on the edge of the group, was sucked through it and out of sight.

'But Addie, the place is haunted,' protested Darwin.

'Haunted, my — ' Adelaide looked round. 'Where's Frazer?'

'Frazer?' called Darwin.

'Frazer, Frazer, Frazer . . .' repeated the echoes.

Then a high-pitched female voice shrieked, 'Who's Frazer?'

Sydney made for the door. 'If you think I'm staying a moment longer — ' she exclaimed.

Adelaide grabbed her by the beak, shutting her up. 'That's enough, Sydney. Fra . . . zer!'

There was no reply.

'It's vanished, Ronnie,' said Reggie.

Ronnie peered into the rainy darkness. 'It's around here somewhere. It must be.'

'Yeah,' said Reggie. 'But where?'

Just above their heads, the Pom hovered in the darkness, chuckling quietly to itself.

Frazer found himself in a long, dark corridor. Still clutching his candle, he followed it into some kind of lumber-room. It was a dark, spooky-looking place, full of strange half-hidden shapes.

'Shocking weather,' said a very British voice from somewhere above his head. 'Absolute shower!'

Frazer looked up. Hanging upside-down from the roof was a ghostly figure. It was white and semi-transparent. But reassuringly, it was a bat, much like himself. It wore a white nightshirt and a monocle, and it had a bushy moustache.

'Jolly different from dear old Oz, I imagine,' said the apparition chattily. 'By the way, I'm Raymond.'

Frazer gulped. 'You're – a ghost!'

'Been one for years – but I'm still Raymond. You're

73

young Frazer, aren't you? From Gulla something or other, eh?'

'Gullagaloona!' whispered Frazer. 'How did you know?'

'Haven't the remotest idea, old boy. Some sort of ghostly perk, I expect. We're relatives, you know.'

Frazer swallowed. 'Relatives?'

'You're my cousin's great-great-great-great-great-great grandson. He said he was a skipper on a convict ship – personally, I think he was a passenger!' A little awkwardly, Raymond polished his monocle. 'The thing is, old chap, I've had an absolutely frightful time – which is why I brought you here.'

'You did?'

'You see, I've got a squatter. Had the whole bally place to myself till about a year ago. And then, quite suddenly, out of the blue, soon as say knife, tiddly-poo – *she* moved in!'

'She?'

'Ghastly creature! Never stops moaning.'

'Why don't you get rid of her, Raymond? You're a ghost – scare the living daylights out of her!'

'Can't old boy – she hasn't got any.'

'You mean – she's dead?'

'As a doornail, old boy. Ghosts can't frighten each other, you see. Simply not done. That's why I need someone from your side of the grave, as it were.'

There was a distant moaning sound. Raymond looked worried. So did Frazer. 'Did you hear something?'

'Could have been the wind,' said Raymond uneasily. 'Does it worry you?'

'Only after too many bananas,' said Frazer.

'Good show, Frazer. I knew I could rely on you.'

'What for, Raymond?'

'To get rid of *her* for me – my squatter.'

Frazer swallowed hard. 'Me?' he said faintly.

Chapter Ten

The Unwilling Exorcists

Outside Philthy Place the Winjin' Pom hung suspended over the Crows' sinister black limousine. Ronnie peered out into the stormy darkness. 'Rain's still heavy,' he said.

Above him, the Pom muttered, 'It's going to get a lot heavier,' as he dropped like a stone, crushing the car below.

Rising quickly off the wreckage, the Pom dropped back on to the drive and drove himself away. 'I'm off to find a nice garridge,' he grunted. 'Weather like this ain't fit for van nor beast.'

The Pom disappeared into the darkness.

Inside the hall, Adelaide was trying to organize a search-party. 'OK, I'll look upstairs. Darwin, you look in the cellar.'

Darwin turned to Sydney. 'Couldn't you look in the cellar?'

'I'm not looking anywhere!'

'Listen, you dill-brains,' said Adelaide. 'Do you want to find Frazer or not?'

'Not if he's in the cellar!' said Darwin frankly.

'Whee!' yelled Bruce, as he slid down the banisters. He arrived at the bottom and looked round. 'No sign of Frazer upstairs. I reckon he's been got.'

'Got?' quavered Sydney.

'Yeah!' said Bruce with gruesome relish. 'He's probably one of the living dead by now.'

Darwin shuddered. 'Living dead? You mean – he's been turned into a Pom?'

A terrible screech rang out. The Aussies watched in horror as a vase lifted itself from the mantelpiece and smashed against the wall.

'We're trapped!' sobbed Sydney.

With a terrifying screech the ghostly white form of a bat, a female one this time, materialized above them and floated across the room.

'Let's get going,' said Adelaide at last.

The terrified Aussies headed towards the door.

In the lumber-room Frazer was saying, 'But I don't know anything about exorcism, Raymond.'

'Nothing to it, old boy. You just need some garlic and a stake.'

'Steak?' said Frazer indignantly. 'I'm a fruit-bat!'

'A wooden stake, old boy.'

'That's for vampires.'

'Is it? How absolutely sickening! What does one do with spirits?'

'Haven't a clue, Raymond. I'm teetotal.'

With a blood-curdling wail the door burst open and the glowing white form of a female bat flitted towards them.

'It's her,' sobbed Raymond. 'She's found me. I'm doomed!'

Down below, the Aussies were listening in horror to the racket from upstairs. Screams and yells, the sound of hurled furniture and smashing crockery, all mingled with the howling of the wind and the crashing of the thunder.

'Something horrible's happening up there,' said Sydney.

Then they heard a familiar voice yell, 'Aaaargh!'

'That was Frazer!' said Adelaide.

'His fate is sealed,' sobbed Sydney.

At that moment everything went quiet.

The secret panel in the wall opened, and Frazer emerged, accompanied by his ghostly companion. Sydney took one look at the ghost and dived for her bucket – only to find Darwin there before her.

'My bucket, I think, Darwin,' she said acidly, snatching it off his head, and plunging her own inside.

Darwin took one look at Raymond and keeled over backwards. Adelaide blenched but managed to stand her ground.

Frazer did the honours. 'Addie, this is Raymond. Raymond, Addie.'

'Charmed,' said Raymond smoothly.

'And just short of square leg we have Sydney – she's checking the safety apparatus,' continued Frazer. 'And Darwin – he's having a little lie-down.' Bruce suddenly dropped down from the ceiling. 'And here's Brucie.'

'Can I bite 'im?'

Frazer shook his head. 'Raymond's a relative of mine. He's got a problem.'

Adelaide looked at – or rather through – Raymond. 'I can see that,' she remarked.

'Raymond,' said Frazer. 'You're batting.'

'Well, you see,' began Raymond, 'I've got this squatter . . .'

Sydney took her head out of her bucket and Darwin came to.

'He wants us to cancel the fixture, as it were,' explained Frazer.

'Us? How?'

'Exorcism!' whispered Frazer.

'Frazer – none of us knows the first thing about exorcism,' said Adelaide.

Suddenly the ghostly form of the female bat appeared behind Raymond. 'You miserable spectre!' it screeched.

'Now just hold it a mo!' ordered Adelaide.

The ghost gave Adelaide an icy stare. 'Ai don't think we've met,' she said, in a cut-glass county accent.

It took more than a snobbish ghost to intimidate Adelaide. 'Don't you come it with me, you flaky old ghoul,' she declared loudly.

'Yeah,' said Sydney, gathering her courage. 'Go and find your own place to haunt.'

'Rack off, you spooky old squatter!' squeaked Bruce.

'Squatter?' The lady ghost was outraged. 'Squatter! I'm his wife! I've been married to him for a hundred and twenty-two years.'

Frazer turned to Raymond. 'Is this true?'

'Ah well,' sighed Raymond – and vanished.

'Raymond!' snapped his ghostly wife.

'Raymond's got a problem.'

Obediently, Raymond reappeared. 'Yes, Mavis, my dear?'

'Have you been trying to get me exorcized again?'

'My dear old thingy . . .'

Mavis turned to the Aussies. 'Oh, he's always doing it!'

'Is he?' said Frazer blankly.

'It won't work, Raymond,' said Mavis fiercely. 'If I've told you once, I've told you a thousand times – I'm staying!'

Suddenly Raymond shot off, Mavis in hot pursuit. As the ghosts battled, a storm of psychic energy was unleashed.

All kinds of domestic objects were snatched up and sent swirling round the room. Cups and saucers, pots and pans, a gas stove, an oven, a kitchen sink. Even the Pom passed through the room, muttering, 'Anyone see a garridge?'

'Raymond!' screeched Mavis, hurling a TV set at him. 'Come here.'

'You can't throw for toffee,' jeered Raymond. 'You never could!'

'I'll give you exorcism!' shouted Mavis, hurling an oven.

Raymond dodged nimbly. 'If you threw a party you'd miss!'

'I think it's time to go,' said Sydney.

'Yeah, family schemozzle,' said Darwin. 'Nothing to do with us.'

The Pom reappeared, going the other way. 'If I don't find a garridge soon I'll have an accident.'

'Why on earth did I marry you?' moaned Mavis.

'Because no one else was stupid enough to marry *you*!'

'Shall we go?' suggested Darwin.

Adelaide was strangely reluctant. 'Wait a mo. It isn't exorcism they need. It's *counselling*. Marriage guidance. I did some back in Gullagaloona.' She turned to Sydney. 'Remember the Possums, Darlene and Les? They were at daggers drawn – until I counselled 'em.'

'What happened after that?' asked Darwin.

'They got divorced,' said Sydney.

'You can't counsel spirits,' said Frazer.

'Perhaps they should start a family?' suggested Darwin.

'Bit late for that,' said Adelaide.

'I dunno – what about phantom pregnancies?'

Adelaide raised her voice. 'Mavis! Raymond!'

As the psychic storm died away, the battling ghosts reappeared. An axe floated past Raymond and a chainsaw by Mavis, but they were too tired to make use of them.

'I'm absolutely knackered,' panted Raymond.

'It's time you two were sorted out,' said Adelaide determinedly.

A few minutes later, Adelaide had everyone gathered around a big table. 'Now then,' she began in her best caring voice. 'Let's talk things through, calmly and rationally. Which of you died first?'

'He did,' said Mavis.

Raymond nodded. 'It was such a relief. I thought I was finally free of her. But I was tied to haunting the house – I couldn't get past the front door.'

Mavis said icily, 'You didn't have to haunt *me* as well!'

Darwin was amazed. '*You* haunted Mavis?'

'A fatal mistake,' admitted Raymond. 'She died of fright.'

'And that brought you together again,' said Sydney.

'Eternally,' said Raymond bitterly.

'So now you just have to make the best of it, don't you?' said Adelaide. 'Now, where did things go wrong? Mavis, you first.'

'On our honeymoon. I caught him hibernating in the bathroom.'

'Now that was a little selfish of you, Raymond,' reproved Sydney.

'I'm doing the counselling,' snarled Adelaide, dropping the caring voice. 'So shut yer gob.'

'We all want to help Mavis and Raymond just as much as you do,' said Sydney primly. 'Don't we, Darwin?'

Darwin had nodded off. 'What? Er, yeah.'

'Oh, you're such a wimp, Darwin,' accused Adelaide.

Bruce dropped down over the table squeaking, 'Wimp! Wimp! Wimp! Darwin's a wimp!'

'Shut up you little creep!' bellowed Darwin.

'Brucie can't help how he walks, Darwin,' protested Frazer. 'You'll give him a complex.'

'I'll give him a right-hander,' muttered Adelaide.

'Fine counsellor you make!' sneered Sydney. 'You couldn't even keep your own husband!'

'At least I've had one, you flightless freak,' yelled Adelaide.

'Now, let's talk things over calmly and rationally,' urged the ghostly Raymond.

'Rack off!' bawled Adelaide, and the offended ghosts vanished.

'I'm going straight home to mother,' announced Sydney. 'As for you, Adelaide, I never want to see you again as long as I live!'

'Well, that suits me!'

'Let's go, everybody,' said Sydney, heading for the door. As she reached the door it swung open, revealing the Crows.

'Surprise, surprise!' said Reggie.

'Long time no see,' said Ronnie.

'Bin keeping well 'ave we?' asked Reggie.

Ten minutes later the Aussies were trussed up like turkeys. Adelaide and Sydney were tied to one chair, Frazer and Darwin to another. The two chairs had been set back to back, and bound together with a huge coil of rope.

Bruce was in the middle, stuck up where the two chair backs came together. He was completely helpless too – all his eight legs had been tied together above his head.

'All right,' said Reggie. 'Where is it?'

'Where's what?' quavered Sydney.

'The Winjin' Pom,' said Ronnie.

'Outside,' said Frazer.

Reggie shook his head. 'I beg to differ.'

'You better tell us,' said Ronnie.

'Or we put the kibosh on little nasty here,' said Reggie.

Ronnie produced a large and sinister-looking aerosol can. the label bore a skull and crossbones and the word KIBOSH.

'En-vir-on-ment-ally friendly – except to spiders.'

Adelaide refused to be intimidated. 'Listen, you two dills – if the Pom's not outside, we haven't a clue where it is!'

Ronnie brandished the aerosol. 'Shall I give the little squirt a little squirt, Reggie?'

'I'm too young to die!' piped Bruce.

Reggie looked thoughtful. 'I think he's old enough – don't you, Ron?'

'Yeah, course he is.' Ronnie trained the insect spray on Bruce.

'No!' squeaked Bruce. 'If you kill me, you'll never find out where the treasure is!'

Ronnie lowered the can. 'Treasure?'

'Yeah, right, the treasure!' chorused the Aussies.

All except Darwin. 'What treasure's that, then?'

'You're such a wimp, Darwin!' yelled the Aussies.

'Nice try, hairy-legs,' said Reggie. 'Right now, Ronnie here is going to count to ten . . .'

Ronnie frowned. 'Er, Reggie . . .'

'I repeat,' said Reggie. 'Ronnie here is going to count to *five* . . . and if you don't tell us where the Pom is – exit insect!'

'Oh no!' said Bruce pathetically.

Raymond materialized behind the Crow brothers.

'One . . .' said Ronnie.

Mavis materialized beside Raymond.

'Oh, you made me jump!' he complained.

'You're so neurotic, Raymond.'

'Mavis we've got to do something.'

'Why? I hate spiders.'

'Yes, but if they do him in, he could be here for ever.'

Mavis shuddered. 'A spider spook?'

'Worse!' said Raymond. An *Australian* spider spook.'

'What an appalling thought!'

'We can't let it happen, old girl. So, let's get haunting.'

'Four,' said Ronnie.

With fearsome howls, Raymond and Mavis swooped down on the Crows. They chased them round and round the room – and then disappeared.

The Crows stood there quivering in terror – and Raymond and Mavis reappeared, howling ferociously, and drove them out of the door into the rainy night.

'And stay out!' said the right-hand gargoyle.

Reggie and Ronnie looked at it in horror – and fled into the darkness.

'Don't forget to write,' said the gargoyle on the left.

'Super, Raymond!' said Frazer.

'Supernatural, actually, Frazer,' replied Raymond.

Soon they were on the doorstep, saying goodbye to their ghostly hosts. The Pom had reappeared and was ready to go.

'Thank you so much,' said Mavis. 'Raymond has promised not to bring anyone else here to exorcize me – haven't you, Raymond?'

'Absolutely, Mavis, old thing. Only causes unnecessary friction. Well, toodle-pip, chaps.'

'Toodeloo, everyone!' called Mavis.

As the two ghosts faded away, the Aussies looked at each other a little shamefacedly.

'Sydney,' said Adelaide. 'I said some pretty unforgivable things, didn't I?'

'So did I, Addie. And I'm sorry.'

'I'm sorry too, Sydney.'

'What about me?' asked Bruce.

Adelaide nodded sadly. 'I said some pretty terrible things to you, little Brucie, didn't I?'

'Huh!' said Brucie.

'And I said some really horrible things to you, Darwin.'

Darwin looked hurt. 'You called me a wimp.'

'Well, you *are* a wimp,' said everyone.

'But a nice wimp,' said Adelaide.

Darwin was touched. 'Thanks, Addie.'

'So we'll let bygones be has-beens, eh?' said Adelaide.

'Too right,' said Sydney. 'Thanks Addie.'

'And I'd like to thank you too, Addie,' said Frazer.

'Yeah – and I'd like to throw up,' said the Winjin' Pom. 'I hate slushy, sentimental, happy endings.'

Chapter Eleven

Small World

Things were back to normal for the Gullagaloona Backpack-ers. They were in the Winjin' Pom, they were on the road again, and they were being chased by the Crow brothers.

Somehow Reggie and Ronnie had recovered from their supernatural fright, got their crushed car repaired and picked up their trail. Sydney craned her neck to look at the sinister black shape behind them. 'They're gaining on us!' she screamed.

'Is this the best you can do, Pom?' demanded Adelaide.

'You tell me – you're driving,' snarled the Pom.

Frazer gave a sudden yell of alarm. They were heading straight towards a ROAD CLOSED barrier.

The Aussies squawked – and the Pom sighed wearily, extended his door-wings and heaved himself off the ground. Clearing the barrier by inches, he heaved himself into the sky. The pursuing limousine screeched to a halt.

'Oh dear,' said Ronnie Crow. 'It's done it again, Reggie.'

Reggie was busy with an expensive camera – nicked from one of the best shops in Oxford Street – and was taking shot after shot of the flying Pom.

Click . . . click . . . click . . . One by one the shots of the soaring Pom were being projected on a viewing screen in Jay Gee's office. Jay Gee blinked hooded filmy eyes. 'Is it a bird? Is it a plane?' he croaked. 'No! It's Super Van!' Howard cackled with hyena laughter.

Jay Gee's throaty whisper cut him off. 'Get me the Crows!'

'To hear is to obey, Jay Gee.' Reluctantly for once, Howard scurried to the phone. After his failed assassination attempt and his disastrous trip in the *non*-flying camper, he had fled back to Jay Gee. He'd hoped he'd seen the last of the Crows.

When the call came through, Ronnie and Reggie were on their terrace, overlooking Trafalgar Square. Ronnie had a row of cuddly toys lined up on the parapet, and was happily tipping them over, one by one. It would have been more fun with Howard, but he seemed to have disappeared.

The mobile phone rang. Reggie picked it up. 'Crow's Nest – Reggie speaking.'

'OK, I got the picture.'

Reggie gulped. 'Jay Gee?'

'Who else?' wheezed the unmistakable voice. 'I'm making you an offer you can't refuse. Get me the camper, and you're off the hook. You got twenty-four hours.'

Covering the earpiece, Reggie looked across at his brother.

'It's Jay Gee – he says we've got twenty-four hours.'

Ronnie tipped a teddy bear over the edge. 'Tell him we need a day at least.'

'It's a bit tight, Jay Gee,' said Reggie.

'Twenty-four hours,' said the remorseless whisper. 'Or it's beaks in the blender time!'

Reggie put down the phone. 'He's beside himself.'

Ronnie prepared a fluffy bunny for the high-jump. 'That's good, Reggie – I thought he'd be angry.'

Slamming down the phone, Jay Gee sat brooding. Those Limey Crows would screw things up for sure. There was only one answer.

'Howard? We're going to England.'

Free of cares, for the moment at least, the Aussies were driving away from Sellafield Power Station, discussing their visit.

'The outside looks just like the National Theatre,' said Sydney.

'Only the inside was more entertaining,' said Adelaide.

'Marvellously clean, though, wasn't it?' said Darwin.

Sydney flourished her fan. 'I've never seen a floor so highly polished.'

'Well,' said Darwin, who was naturally gullible, 'I feel so much more reassured about atomic power.'

Sydney leaned across. 'It's not safe, you know,' she whispered. Darwin looked worried. 'Atomic power?'

'No – that floor! You could slip and do yourself an injury.'

Frazer was dozing quietly in the back of the Pom. Bruce dropped down in front of him and squeaked 'Fraze! *Fraze!*'

'Howzat!' said Frazer, waking with a start. 'What's up, Brucie?'

'I don't feel too clever, Brucie. I think I'm gonna chuck up!'

'I *told* you not to go off on your own, Brucie.'

'As one reactor said to the other,' giggled Bruce.

'You may have been exposed to low-level radiation.'

'I hope so, Fraze! Do I look any bigger? I saw this film, right? About radioactive ants and they got *huge*!'

'Size isn't everything, Brucie,' said Frazer reprovingly.

'Yeah, but think of it, Fraze,' said Bruce excitedly. 'Crashing me way round Melbourne the size of a seven-four-seven, crunching up petrol tankers. No one'll flush me down the plug-hole then!'

Spurred on by Jay Gee's threats, the Crows too were on the road. Their starling informers had spotted the van near Sellafield.

Ronnie tore along the narrow lane, well over the speed limit, missing a Sellafield delivery lorry by inches.

'You'll lose your licence one day,' said Reggie.

'No one is ever gonna take a licence away from me,' said Ron.

'Only 'cos you ain't got one.'

Suddenly the Crows saw the Pom just ahead. 'We got 'em this time!' said Ronnie.

At the same moment Adelaide saw the black car in her rear-view mirror. 'Oh no, it's the Crows!' She put her foot down but the Pom refused to move any faster.

'Get cracking, yer shonky old no-hoper!' screeched Adelaide.

The Crows were catching up.

'Why doesn't he fly?' sobbed Sydney.

'I'll fly when I feel like it,' muttered the Pom.

The Crows' limousine drew level, and Reggie stuck his head out of the window. 'Pull over,' he snarled.

Adelaide snatched up a smelly old pullover from the seat and tossed it neatly over his head.

'Very funny!' Reggie disentangled himself. 'Right, Ronnie.'

The limousine passed the Pom and drew ahead, preparing to block the road. The Pom braked to a sudden halt. The black car sped on.

'Er, Reggie?' said Ronnie, pointing ahead.

Reggie, who had been looking over his shoulder, turned round. A massive lorry was heading straight towards them, completely filling the narrow lane.

'Aaaargh!' said the Crow brothers in unison.

Ronnie spun the wheel, crashing through a gate into a field.

'Mind the gate, Ronnie.'

'What gate, Reg?'

Behind them, the Pom made a sudden right turn and swerved through a tall gateway, parking with a screech of brakes in the yard beyond.

The Pom looked round. 'Well, weld me rigid.'

They were in a scrapyard, battered cars and bits of cars all around. The whole place had an air of rust and gloomy decay. To the Pom it was a bit like hiding out in a cemetery – but it would have to do.

'We'll have to lie low for a bit,' he announced, parking in a gap between an old bus and a rusty van.

Sydney stared disdainfuly at the piles of rusting metal. 'Here?'

'Got no choice,' grunted the Pom.

The door to the yard swung closed. There was a notice on it. When they drove in, the notice had been hidden because the gate was swung back against the wall. Now the notice was on the outside, so they still couldn't see it. It said CARS CRUSHED WHILE YOU WAIT.

Suddenly the Aussies heard a strange grinding, clanking noise. There was the rattle of a heavy chain, a clang as something struck the roof – and suddenly they were rising upwards, swinging through the air.

'What is it?' yelled Adelaide. 'What's going on?'

'I feel sick,' complained Darwin as the van swung to and fro.

They had been picked up by the grabber of a giant crane, and they were being swung over to the crushing chamber.

They could see it below them now, a terrifying glowing red pit. The crane lowered them down towards it . . .

'Time to bale out, Frazer!' yelled Bruce. 'I'm getting out of here!' With a yell of 'Geronimo!' he jumped through the open window.

For the Pom and the rest of the Aussies it was too late.

The Crows drew up in the yard and looked up – just in time to see the Pom being lowered into the crushing chamber.

'We've gotta stop it!' yelled Reggie.

Ronnie shouted up at the crane operator. 'Oi, you! You are crushing our camper!'

Ignoring them, the crane operator opened the grabber. The Pom dropped, disappearing inside the crushing chamber. The massive metal lid slammed down.

The Pom and the Aussies were bathed in a sinister red light.

'We're about to be tinned,' screamed Adelaide.

'Looks like the end of the innings,' said Frazer with the quiet dignity of a true cricketer.

The Pom closed its bulging eyes and concentrated – hard. Crackling energy, like multicoloured lightning, sparked and sizzled around it . . . Then everything went quiet.

'It's broken down,' whispered Adelaide.

'Oh no it ain't,' rumbled the Pom.

There was a mechanical clanking sound and they started moving jerkily forward.

'We're moving!' said Sydney.

'Course we are,' said the Pom. 'We're on the conveyor belt.'

They moved down some kind of tunnel towards a metal door. As they reached it the door slid up and the conveyor belt shot them out into the open air.

The crane lowered them towards the crushing chamber.

They landed with a bump beside something massive and circular. Before they could work out what it was a huge, hairy shape loomed over them. A deep voice growled, 'Hey, Fraze, I must've mutated! Said I'd get bigger, didn't I?' It was a giant Bruce!

It was Adelaide who understood what had happened. She looked at the huge round object and realized it was an abandoned tyre – a tyre that now looked as big as a building.

'Pom!' she said accusingly. 'Have you done what I think you've done?'

The Pom looked smug. 'Could be,' he agreed.

'You've shrunk us.'

'Ten out of ten. Give the lady a goldfish.'

'You steaming great nong!' shrieked Adelaide.

'Well, thanks for the standing ovation.'

'Well, look at us,' said Adelaide. 'We're minute.'

Sydney stuck her neck outside the Pom, and took in the awful reality. 'What am I going to say to Mother?' she croaked.

'How about "Watch where you're treading, Mum"?' suggested the Pom.

Only Darwin gave the Pom some credit for saving their lives.

'I suppose we really ought to be grateful,' he began.

'Oh, you're such a wimp, Darwin,' snarled Adelaide. 'Is this permanent?' she demanded of the Pom.

'Don't be a berk,' replied the camper.

'OK,' said Adelaide, a little mollified. 'We'll just stay here then. Pom, you can do the getting-big-again bit.'

Nothing happened.

Adelaide tapped her foot. '*When* you're ready, Pom.'

'OK,' said the Pom sleepily. 'When I'm ready.'

'Well? When *will* you be ready?'

'In about twelve hours.'

'Twelve hours!' gasped Sydney.

The Pom yawned. 'Happens automatically.'

'Why can't it happen automatically now?' asked Darwin mildly.

'I gotter get me strength back, don't I? I mean, what do you take me for? Chitty Chitty Bang Bang?'

'We *can't* stay here,' protested Adelaide. 'We'll have a crushed car landing on top of us!'

Above them they heard the rumble of the crusher. Adelaide tried to start the engine but nothing happened. 'Do start up, Pom!'

'Do me a favour,' moaned the Pom wearily. 'I'm Kerry Packered! Me battery's flatter than a motorway hedgehog.'

'We'll have to push him,' said Frazer.

'Again,' said Adelaide bitterly.

As Adelaide opened the door a huge shadow fell. Looming over her was a giant Reggie Crow. Adelaide slammed the door. With giant Crows about, it was safer inside.

Reggie bent down and picked up the camper.

'What's that, then?' asked Ronnie.

Reggie was staring hard at the miniature Pom. 'Stone me! I do not believe it!'

Still carrying the little van he got back in the car.

Ronnie peered over his shoulder. 'Looks a bit like that camper, don't it?'

'It *is* the camper, Ronnie.'

'Er, no, Reggie. The camper's bigger than that.'

'Ron,' said Reggie urgently. '*It is the camper and they are all inside it.*'

'Nah,' said Ronnie. 'They couldn't all get in there, Reg.'

'Have a butcher's,' said his brother.

Ronnie peered through the windscreen. 'Blimey! It *is* them! Ain't they gone little! 'Ere, where's the spider then, eh?' He gave the van a shake.

'Kindly refrain, Ronnie,' said Reggie, snatching back the van. 'He's in there somewhere.'

'Jay Gee'll be pleased,' said Ronnie. 'He can take it home in his suitcase.'

Reggie slammed the car door. 'Gotta do a bit of thinking, Ronnie.'

'Have I, Reggie?'

'Not you, Ron. I've told you before. Don't think and drive.'

'Yeah, right.'

Ronnie started the engine and drove away.

In the back window of the Crows' car hung a pair of

'Blimey! Ain't they gone little!'

white fluffy dice. Close by, on the back window ledge, crouched a black furry spider.

'This looks like a job for spiderman,' whispered Bruce to himself.

Chapter Twelve

Ronnie's Pets

The Crow brothers were riding up in their lift. Reggie was carrying the Pom. He was also, although he didn't know it, carrying Bruce, who was crouching on his shoulder.

Ronnie tried to snatch the camper from his brother.

'Behave,' said Reggie severely, pulling it back.

Ronnie peered delightedly into the camper. 'Ah, look . . . they're just the size of my little finger,' he crooned.

Reggie carried the van out of the lift.

'Mind what you're doing,' urged Ronnie. 'Don't shake them up.'

'They'll be all right,' said Reggie, 'I'll put them over here.'

Ronnie tried to grab the van. 'No, I want 'em over here.'

Inside the camper the Aussies were bouncing off the walls.

'No, Ronnie,' said Reggie firmly. 'We're going to put them on this table here.'

'Tip 'em out, then,' urged Ronnie. 'I want to look at them.'

'Later, Ronnie.'

'Go on! I want to play with them now!'

'Well, you ain't going to.'

'Fair do's, Ronnie. They're half mine anyway.'

'What do you mean, half yours?' said Reggie indignantly. 'Who found 'em, eh? Who found 'em?'

Ronnie hung his head. 'You did, Reggie.'

'Well then.'

'Just for five minutes,' pleaded Ronnie.

'Not after what you did to our train set.'

'I only stopped the engine, Reggie.'

'With a hammer, Ronnie.'

'I'll be ever so gentle with them. I just want to make 'em run around a bit.'

'No,' said Reggie firmly. 'It'll be just like your other toys. In five minutes they'd be all over the floor with their heads chewed off.'

Ronnie looked guilty. 'Please, Reggie. We could have races and everything.'

The telephone rang. Reggie answered it reluctantly.

'Oh, Jay Nice,' he babbled. 'How very Gee to hear from you!'

Jay Gee looked at the phone and shook his head. 'I'm upset,' he said with gentle menace. 'You haven't been in touch. What gives with the camper?'

'Well, it's . . . it's . . .'

Ronnie's voice came over the phone. 'It's here.'

'So I can pick it up?'

Ronnie snatched the phone. 'You can pick it up wiv one hand!'

Reggie grabbed the phone back. 'Er . . . what time will you be gracing us with your charming presence, Jay Gee?'

'Eight o'clock, your time. Have the camper ready – or else.'

Inside the Pom, Adelaide peered out of the window. 'They've gone,' she announced.

There was a knocking at the back door.

'Who's that?' asked Sydney nervously.

'Me!' said a deep gruff voice.

'It's little Brucie,' said Frazer delightedly.

He opened the back door and little Brucie, who seemed as big as an elephant to the shrunken Aussies, squeezed his furry bulk inside.

'Anything to eat?' he giggled. 'Apart from you lot!'

The others stared at him in alarm.

'Uh oh! I think I'm gonna sneeze,' he grinned.

'You can't stay in here, Bruce,' protested Adelaide.

'Why not?'

'They're just isn't room for you, Brucie,' explained Frazer.

'I've as much right to be in here as any of ya!'

'Do you mind taking your leg out of my fire-bucket?' said Sydney.

Bruce burped, and the Aussies rocked in the blast.

'Oh no, fair play, Bruce,' wailed Frazer.

'Ooh, we're stuck like this, I know we are!' screamed Sydney.

Adelaide gave her a disgusted look. 'Don't *perform*, Sydney!'

'How can we get back to Oz when our tickets are bigger than we are? What if he can't expand again?'

The Pom's rumbling voice filled the camper. 'Cobblers! 'Course I can, I done it before. Happens twelve hours after the shrinking, to the second.'

(Just below the Pom's eyeline, Reggie and Ronnie were crouched under the table, listening eagerly.)

'How can you be so sure?' demanded Adelaide.

'Because the TDC in the compression stroke is reached in each cylinder when the next but two cylinders in ignition order have their valves overlappin'.'

Frazer blinked. 'What does that mean?'

'I dunno,' confessed the Pom. 'Sounds good, though, dunnit?'

Adelaide checked her watch. 'Twelve hours – that's eight o'clock tomorrow, right?'

'What about us, though, Pom?' asked Frazer.

'You'll expand too – as long as you're inside.'

'What a relief!' said Reggie. 'Hear that? It's gonna get big again, Ronnie!'

Ronnie nodded. 'So we can give it to Jay Gee, like we said.'

Reggie gave him a cunning look. 'And we can keep the mini-Aussies as pets.'

'But they're going to get big again too, Reggie.'

'*Not if we take 'em out of the Pom, Ronnie.*'

'Why didn't I think of that?'

''Cos you're the thick one, Ronnie.' Reggie gestured expansively. 'It'll be just like *Gulliver's Travels*!'

'Yeah!' said Ronnie. 'Er, what will, Reggie?'

'We'll tour the world with 'em, Ronnie! Make millions! A show this small could be really big.'

'I like it, Reggie.'

Reggie looked serious. 'I've always had a yen for the bright lights, you know, Ronnie.'

''Ere, we ain't giving up crime though, are we?'

'No, we're going where the real villains are, Ronnie.'

'Where's that, Reggie?'

'Showbusiness!'

Later that night, Ronnie came back into the flat clutching an empty cardboard box with holes punched in the side.

'Here we are, Reggie.'

Ronnie leaned over the camper. ''Ullo, little Aussie-Wozzies.'

''Ere, we're talking to you lot,' said Reggie.

Ronnie peered through the window. 'We know you're in there,' he croaked.

'So come on out, eh?' said Reggie.

'Or we're coming in!' said Ronnie.

'OK, if that's 'ow you want to play it,' said Reggie. 'We'll 'ave you out of there in a trice. Ronnie, do the honours.'

Ronnie opened the door of the Pom and picked it up by the bonnet, shaking gently. One by one the Aussies slid helplessly out of the camper, landing in a tangled heap at the bottom of the box.

The Crows peered into the box – not noticing Bruce, who was hiding behind a clock on the mantelpiece.

'Aaah!' said Ronnie sentimentally. 'We ain't gonna hurt you.'

'Co-operate and you'll be OK,' said Reggie. 'But give us any aggro – and it's playtime with Ronnie.' He put the lid on the box.

'What'll we feed 'em on?' asked Ronnie.

'Don't worry, I'll get some pet food.'

'Right,' said Ronnie enthusiastically. 'An' a little bell and a mirror an' one of those wheels . . .'

'Ronnie,' said Reggie sternly. 'Bedtime!'

It was much later that night in the Crows' luxurious bedroom. Reggie was in one of the twin beds, reading a financial magazine. In the other bed, Ronnie was leaning over to peer into the box, which rested on a table between the beds. 'I love that little fat one,' he murmured.

Reggie put down his magazine and switched out the light. 'Ronnie – go to sleep.'

Obediently, Ronnie lay down, pulling the duvet over his head.

It was pretty dark inside the box, though a few rays of light came through the air-holes.

Adelaide looked round the sad little group. 'Looks like we've come a bit of a gutzer.'

Sydney, as usual, was almost hysterical. 'Are we supposed to spend the rest of our lives in an egg box? Jumping through paper hoops for a couple of psychotic screwballs?'

'Oh, stop flapping your gums, and listen,' said Adelaide. 'We've got to get back inside the Pom before eight – but if we get back in the Pom up here, they're sure to find us.'

'She's not wrong,' said Darwin. 'So what do we do, Addie?'

'Listen,' said Adelaide. 'The Crows won't let the Pom get big up here, will they?'

'Wouldn't do their table much good,' agreed Frazer.

'So!' said Adelaide triumphantly. 'They'll take it down to the garage – and that's where we get back in!' Unzipping her never-failing pouch, she produced a saw and set to work.

It didn't take too long to make a large circular hole in the cardboard box, even though she had to work quietly for fear of waking the Crows. When the circle was complete she pushed it free – and found herself staring at the giant Bruce.

'I was sweating on you getting out,' he said.

'I bet you were.' Adelaide climbed through the hole, followed by Sydney, Frazer and Darwin. They found themselves on a polished plain – the top of the Crows' bedside table.

'This way,' said Bruce and led them to the edge.

They peered over. It looked a very long way down.

Sydney gasped. 'We'll never get down there!'

'No worries,' said Frazer. 'I'll fly down.'

'I can't,' said Sydney. 'I haven't got the wings for it.'

'And I haven't the stomach,' said Darwin miserably.

Frazer looked worried. 'We can't leave you up here.'

'You won't have to,' said Bruce. 'Watch!' He ran three times round Reggie's cocoa mug, spinning his thread, then dashed to the edge and sprang off. 'Geronimo!'

He slid down the thread and looked up. 'Now climb down me thread!'

Darwin backed away. 'I can't do that, it'll break.'

'No it won't, Darwin.'

'You'll have to help me, Addie . . .'

'OK, just watch, I'll go first.'

With the courage of a born leader, Adelaide clenched her teeth, closed her eyes, and slid down Bruce's giant thread to the floor. She looked up and waved. 'See, Darwin?'

Still Darwin hung back. 'I'd sooner stay up here,' he muttered.

'OK! But remember, you're Ronnie's favourite.'

'Oh yeah,' said Darwin miserably. Gritting his teeth, he grabbed the thread – and landed quite unhurt beside Adelaide.

'Now, ace it up, Sydney!' called Adelaide.

Sydney couldn't resist a last dramatic scene, 'Frazer, if I don't make it – will you, will you – break the news to Mother?' She put the handle of her fire-bucket in her beak, and jumped . . .

Adelaide watched from below. 'Move yourself, Darwin!'

Darwin blinked at her. 'Why, Addie?'

His question was answered when Sydney landed on top of him.

She picked herself up, and retrieved the fire-bucket.

'That was a nice soft landing,' she smiled happily.

'They don't come much softer than Darwin,' agreed Adelaide, looking down at the prostrate wombat.

'Ah, the dear thing broke my fall,' gushed Sydney.

'I wonder what else he broke,' said Adelaide, hauling Darwin to his feet.

Frazer spread his wings and glided smoothly down to join them.

Adelaide led them out of the room, and paused on the threshold. Ahead of them stretched acres of fitted carpet, as high as jungle grass. 'Come on,' she said. 'Let's find that lift!'

Jay Gee was winging his way across the ocean – not personally, of course, but in his custom-made private jet, Godfather One. He sat in one of a pair of fat armchairs in the main cabin. On one side of Jay Gee was a bottle of champagne in an ice bucket, on the other his wind-up gramophone was playing an ancient 78 of an amazingly screechy soprano.

Opposite him sat Howard, an expression of agony on his face and a soft cushion jammed against each ear.

The plane flew on . . .

It was early next morning and the frantic Crows were searching for the missing Aussies. By now they were running around in circles.

'They ain't in the bathroom!' reported Ronnie.

'They ain't in the kitchen!' said Reggie.

'They've gone, Reggie,' sobbed Ronnie. 'They've got out!'

Reggie had a sudden inspiration. 'Check the Pom! Check the Pom!'

Ronnie snatched up the Pom and peered inside. 'I can't see 'em . . . We've lost 'em!'

The bell rang. The Crows looked at the ornate wall-clock. It was five to eight.

'Jay Gee!' they moaned together.

From behind a bookcase close to the lift, the Aussies waited tensely.

Ronnie snatched up the Pom, the lift doors opened and Howard appeared. He greeted the Crows warmly – best to let bygones be bygones, safer too. 'Ronnie, baby, great to see you! Hi, Reggie poos!'

Reggie stepped back, dodging the embrace. 'Where's Jay Gee?'

'He's down in the limo. We didn't see any – ' Howard saw the miniaturized Pom, ' – camper,' he concluded.

'You're not going to believe this, Howard,' began Reggie.

'Oh, I'm trying, I'm trying, fellas!'

Ronnie held up the camper. 'This is it.'

Howard's eyes widened. 'Are you telling me that Jay Gee has flown four thousand miles for *this*?'

Ronnie gulped. 'It shrank.'

'Come on, fellas! I mean, I know you get lots of rain over here, but . . .'

Reggie got a grip on himself. 'I assure you, Howard, it is going to grow again.'

'Grow again?'

Ronnie looked anxiously at the clock. It was a few minutes to eight. 'Er, Reggie,' he warned.

Reggie looked at the clock and gasped. 'We don't want it to do it in the lift!'

Reggie and Ronnie dashed for the lift. Howard hurried after them. So did the miniature Aussies. Fortunately, Howard was still distracting the Crows. 'Fellas, fellas! What's going on?' he called.

'Shut it, Howard,' said Ronnie.

'Hit the fast button!' yelled Reggie.

'Right,' said Ronnie.

He hit the fast button and the lift dropped like a stone.

'That's the one!' said Reggie. The lift doors opened. The Crows and Howard shot out – and so did the Aussies, dodging three pairs of enormous feet.

Jay Gee's limo was parked opposite the lift, next to the Crows' own car. The black glass of the rear passenger door slid down, revealing Jay Gee's sinister face.

'Where is it?' he wheezed.

'Er, Ronnie, would you care to do the honours?'

Dumbly Ronnie held out the little camper.

Jay Gee looked at it. He looked at Ronnie and Reggie.

'Boys,' he whispered menacingly. 'I'm too old to have a sense of humour.' The muzzle of a sub-machine-gun poked out of the window.

The Crows ducked behind the quaking Howard.

'No, Jay Gee, wait!' pleaded Ronnie.

'We can explain,' said Reggie.

'Don't do it, Jay Gee,' sobbed Ronnie.

'Move your butt, Howard,' whispered Jay Gee. 'While you still have a butt to move.'

Howard leaped clear of the Crows – who backed away until they were flattened against their own car.

By now the Aussies were hiding behind the car's front wheel. Adelaide looked longingly at the Pom, still in Ronnie's hands.

'Put it down, you drongo,' she whispered. '*Put it down!*'

'It's gonna get big again, Jay Gee,' babbled Reggie.

'Back to what it was!' promised Ronnie.

'Maybe even bigger!' screamed Reggie.

Even Jay Gee couldn't help being impressed by the sincerity in their voices. Could these Limey loonies be telling the truth?

Ronnie put the Pom down and stepped back.

'Now!' screamed Adelaide. The Aussies ran across the expanse of pitted, oil-stained concrete, heading for the camper.

Luckily they were out of Jay Gee's eyeline. The danger was that the Crows would see them.

They got nearer the camper, nearer . . .

At the last moment the Crows spotted them.

'It's them!' yelled Reggie.

'Let's gettem!' growled Ronnie.

It was then that little Brucie came up trumps. As the Crow brothers moved to grab the escapers, he dropped from the ceiling, yo-yo-ing up and down in front of their astonished faces.

'Gonna bite ya! Gonna bite ya!'

The Crows yelled and ducked – and Frazer, Adelaide, Darwin and Sydney made it into the van – just as time ran out.

Multicoloured rays of energy streaked from the Pom. It grew and grew and grew till it was full size again and so did the Aussies! The Pom roared into life, and zoomed away in a cloud of smoke.

Bruce jumped up and down inside the back window. 'As Winston Churchill said after the Battle of Britain – ner, ner, ner-ner, nerrr!'

The Pom shot up the ramp, out of the garage and disappeared. Jay Gee's cold eyes, more terrifying than his machine-gun, targeted on the terrified Crows. 'I gotta have that camper,' he rasped.

The Pom sped along the road out of London. In the driving seat were all the Aussies, back to normal size.

For once the Pom was in a good mood. 'With one mighty leap, our hero was free. Turning to their gallant rescuer, everyone said — ' The Pom paused hopefully.

The Aussies looked at one other. 'Thanks, Pom!'

'That's more like it – didn't hurt, did it? I could do with that a bit more often, bit of appreciation, bit of praise . . .'

The Aussies looked at one other again. 'Stop winjin', Pom!'

The Pom sighed. 'That's nice, isn't it? That really is nice!'

Still winjin', he rattled away.

Chapter Thirteen

Where's Addie?

The headline read *MAFIA LAWYER HELD*. The accompanying picture showed a shifty-looking canary in a striped suit. The newspaper lay flat on the blotter on the big desk in Jay Gee's ornate penthouse office. Holding it down with one withered claw, Jay Gee was slashing the picture of the unfortunate lawyer with an open razor, and muttering a string of Italian obscenities about the poor man's mother.

His hyena assistant Howard, hovering deferentially as usual, managed to catch one of the key words. 'Mother coming to stay?' he asked brightly.

Jay Gee gave him a look of loathing. 'Max Canary, my personal attorney. He's the latest tenant in the Big House.'

Howard took a keen interest in real estate. 'Oh, I just knew they'd let the place eventually!'

'He's in gaol, you schmo!' screeched Jay Gee. 'And if he sings, Howard, I'll be in there with him. They'll put me away for — '

Jay Gee's beak dropped open and he went rigid.

The medical screens showing his vital responses immediately froze. The financial read-out screens showing the stockmarket index predicted a crash. 'Warning, Stockmarket Index at danger level,' chanted a calm computer voice.

Howard grabbed the cardiac stimulators from their rack and blasted a few thousand volts into Jay Gee's scrawny chest. The lifeline started peaking again and the stockmarket picked up too. 'All clear, all clear' said the calm voice, and the financial screens moved from CRASH to GAIN. With Jay Gee, money *was* life . . .

'Are you hearing me, Howard?' said the revived vulture.

'Oh, I'm hearing you, Jay Gee, honest. Every word. Er, what was that last bit again?'

Jay Gee ripped the paper to shreds with his withered talons. 'Max Canary, ya dumb hyena. I want him rubbed out!'

'How are you gonna do that, Jay Gee?'

Jay Gee was staring into space. 'The Winjin' Pom,' he whispered at last. 'Get me the Winjin' Pom!'

It was night in the woods. The Pom was parked in a secluded glade. Two familiar shapes rose from behind a bush. They ducked down again. Inside the Pom the Aussies were fast asleep. All except Adelaide, who was sitting up in her hammock reading *The Liberated Wallaby's Guide to Car Maintenance*. She yawned . . . Frazer, Darwin and Sydney were stretched out on the main bed. Darwin was tossing and turning, deep in one of his old movie dreams. 'Throw the switches, Igor!' he shouted.

Sydney screamed and sat up.

Darwin dreamed on. 'In fifteen minutes the storm will be at its height,' he droned. 'Doctor Frankenstein's creation will live!' Suddenly he opened his eyes and stared into Sydney's face. She was wearing rollers and face cream. Darwin thought his dream had come alive and gave a yell of alarm. Then, realizing it was only Sydney, he fell back on the pillow and dropped off to sleep.

Just then Adelaide thought she heard someone moving outside. She swung out of her hammock and went to investigate. It was dark and spooky in the woods. Trees rustled in the wind, owls hooted . . .

'Hallo!' called Adelaide. 'Who's there?' There was no reply. Deciding she must have been imagining things, she turned to go back to the Pom. A black shape rose up and grabbed her. She struggled wildly. Suddenly a net was thrown over her *and* her attacker.

'I've got her, Reggie,' yelled Ronnie.

'But you've got me!' Reggie's voice came out of the darkness.

'I know – but at least I know where you are.'

Struggling wildly, Adelaide was carried away.

'Get me the Winjin' Pom!'

At breakfast next morning, the Aussies wondered where she was.

'Maybe she's out jogging,' said Frazer.

'That's it, she's jogging,' said Sydney. 'Pass the Vegemite.'

'Well, I'm worried about her,' said Darwin.

Sydney sighed. 'You're always worried, Darwin. And when you're not, you're worried about not being worried!'

Suddenly a paper-wrapped brick came crashing through the window.

'It's a bomb!' screamed Sydney.

Everyone dived under the table. When there was no explosion they emerged and studied the brick.

'It's not ticking,' said Frazer.

Darwin nodded. 'Sounds more like a brick.'

Slowly Sydney took the paper from the brick. 'It's a note,' she told them.

'What does it say?' asked Darwin nervously.

Sydney read the note aloud. *'Exchange is no robbery. If you want to see your friend again, bring the Winjin' Pom to the United States of America, signed The Crows. PS See map.'*

Frazer looked at the note. 'What map?'

Another brick whizzed through the window.

Sydney unwrapped it and read, *'PPS – This one, stupid. Jay Gee lives here. Land on the White Cross.'*

Godfather One, Jay Gee's private jet, was returning to America. This time its passengers were the Crow brothers, and a furious, bound and gagged Adelaide.

'Why take her?' asked Ronnie. 'We could have got the Pom!'

Reggie looked up from his copy of *The Art of Bullying*. 'Do you fancy flying a clapped-out banger with a mind of its own across the Atlantic?'

'What – now, Reggie?'

'What I am saying is, they're bound to persuade the Pom to rescue her, understood?'

'Oh, I get it, Reggie.'

Reggie looked amazed. 'Really?'

'No, 'course I haven't . . .'
Reggie sighed.

In the woods the Aussies were gathered round the Pom. He wasn't being helpful.

'Rescue her? What do you take me for, the SAS? You'd never get a woolly hat big enough.'

'I know it's a bit of a long way,' said Sydney kindly.

'A bit of a long way? It's four thousand flamin' miles. I wouldn't even make it to Gatwick,' said the Pom crossly.

'You can't let us down,' pleaded Darwin.

'I can let anyone down. I'm an expert.'

Sydney turned to the others with a meaningful look. 'Well, what can you expect? He's a Pom.'

'Wodgermean?' said the Pom suspiciously.

Sydney ignored him. 'If he'd been German or Japanese . . .' she began.

'He'd've been fine,' said Darwin.

'Gutsy!' said Frazer.

'Reliable!' said Sydney.

'Plenty of poke!' piped Bruce.

'Who won the war?' muttered the Pom.

'But no, we had to get a Pom, didn't we? Bunch of time-serving no-hopers,' sniffed Sydney.

'Yeah!' said Bruce, yo-yo-ing up and down on his thread. 'Living in the past and charging admission.'

'That's it!' shouted the Pom. 'You've done it now, you have. Me rad's *boiling*! I'll show you Aussies just what put the great into Britain!'

The Aussies grinned at each other. But now they had to find a way to rescue Adelaide.

'Welcome to America,' whispered Jay Gee with a hideous attempt at a smile.

Adelaide studied the ornate art-deco office, the rows of screens, the Mighty Wurlitzer. She looked at her captors, the terrified Crow brothers, the colourful Howard, above all the horrific old vulture, staring at her malevolently behind his huge desk. Adelaide thought she'd never seen anything more frightening in her life. But she was an Aussie, through and through.

'Get stuffed, you pathetic old parrot!' she snapped.

Howard and the Crows quaked in terror – you just didn't talk to Jay Gee Chicago like that.

Jay Gee himself could hardly take it in. 'Whaaat?' he gasped.

'Listen, you mummified megalomaniac,' said Adelaide, really getting into her stride. 'I know why you've brought me to this over-decorated dunny, but you're going to wish you hadn't.'

'Is that so?'

'Too right, it is. And that goes for the drongo twins and that furry fairy over there!'

'Oh!' simpered Howard, quite flattered.

'Get her out of here!' rasped Jay Gee furiously. The Crows grabbed Adelaide and dragged her out, still yelling and struggling. 'I'll lay one on yer, ya flea-bitten lump of cat food. Boof off the lot of ya!' Jay Gee sighed and turned back to his Mighty Wurlitzer.

Sydney and Frazer sat in the driving cab of the Pom, waiting for Darwin, who had been elected pilot.

Bruce was crouching on the dashboard. 'Why can't I drive?' he demanded.

'You're too young!' snapped Sydney.

'We're not driving, actually, Brucie – we're flying,' said Frazer.

'Actually, Fraze, we ain't even moving,' said Bruce rudely.

Darwin appeared from the back, a Biggles-like figure in goggles, flying helmet and white scarf.

'Come on, Darwin,' said Sydney. 'We haven't got all night!'

'Chocolates away!' said Darwin. 'Er, how do you start it?'

'Turn the key,' said the Pom wearily.

The motor churned sluggishly. 'Come on, Pom!' said Frazer.

'Give us a chance – I'm cold,' said the Pom.

Darwin tried again, the motor churned and coughed.

'Mind me rust!' groaned the Pom. 'It's all that's holding

me together.'

Suddenly the engine coughed into life.

'That's the shot, Pommy!' encouraged Frazer.

'Kick on, cobbers!' piped Bruce.

Darwin looked helplessly at Sydney. 'What do I do now?'

'What gear are you in?'

Darwin looked down at himself. 'Dressing gown, slippers, flying helmet, goggles . . .'

Sydney pointed to the gear-lever and Darwin pulled it. There was a horrid grinding of gears.

'Gordon Bonnet!' groaned the Pom. 'Got me right in the gear box.'

'Depress the clutch, Darwin,' screamed Sydney.

'How?'

Bruce giggled. 'Tell it your life story!'

'Now the gear-lever,' shouted Sydney.

'Nothing's happening,' Darwin said helplessly as he pushed and pulled at the gearstick and frantically trod on all the pedals.

Suddenly the Pom lurched forward. Farting clouds of black smoke, it extended its door-wings, shot down the road and heaved itself inelegantly into the sky. The Aussies cheered, as the Pom soared into the sunset.

'Which way's America?' cried Sydney.

'Ask the Pom,' squeaked Bruce.

'No use asking me,' rumbled the Pom. 'I got no sense of direction whatsoever.'

'Well, just keep going west. Follow your nose,' said Sydney.

'What nose?'

Sydney turned to Darwin. 'Which way, navigator?'

Darwin studied his calculator. 'Twenty-eight degrees, fifteen minutes west north-west . . . Oh, just turn left at the next cloud!'

The Pom soared on through the night sky. Its epic journey was going to set a new record – for the slowest transatlantic flight ever made! It was much, much later. Bruce and Frazer were on watch, Sydney was knitting in the back, Darwin dozed on the bed. Frazer's voice came from the driving cab: 'Land ahoy!'

Sydney poked her head through the curtains. 'At last!' she said dramatically. 'At long last!'

'Yeah, there it is,' said the Pom gloomily. 'Ireland.'

Sydney was outraged. 'But we want America!'

'Well, I got a bit lost,' said the Pom defensively. 'Anyway, I'm going down, I need a rest.'

Darwin did sums on his calculator. 'At this rate, we'll get to America in – four and a half months.'

'Poor Adelaide!' sighed Frazer.

'Hang about,' said the Pom. 'I got an idea!' Suddenly the Pom soared up and up and up. 'Did you bring the anti-freeze?' it shouted. High above the clouds it dropped down and levelled off, bouncing the Aussies around the cabin.

'I'm gonna chuck up,' warned Bruce. 'Look out for the liquid laugh!'

There was a bounce, and it seemed as if the Pom had landed in the clouds. In fact it had come down on top of a jumbo jet. Lowering its wings the Pom settled down to hitch a ride. 'Now, that's what I call plane sailing,' it chuckled.

Some hours later, Frazer popped his head back through the curtain. 'Sydney, Darwin,' he called, 'wake up. We're over America. Time to get ready for the match!'

The Pom extended its stubby wings, took off from the jumbo jet and soared over the lit-up skyscrapers of Chicago. Then it zoomed down amongst them swooping and weaving and spinning like a bee trapped in a bottle.

Sydney studied the map, looking for Jay Gee's white cross amongst the whirling towers. 'This aerial map is impossible,' she complained.

'We'll never see the aerials from up here,' agreed Darwin.

'There it is!' yelled Bruce. 'There it is!'

On a flat roof below them was a large white cross. Suddenly Sydney had a brilliant idea. 'Pom – land on the other building – the one with the circle. If we land on Jay Gee's building, he's got us!'

Cutting its engine, the Pom glided silently down, landing smack in the middle of the circle on the next-door tower.

Darwin patted Sydney on the back. 'Good thinking!'

Sydney tapped her beak. 'Well, you see, Darwin, in this

game you've just got to keep one jump ahead,' she said smugly.

At that moment the Pom started to move. It was going down, quietly and smoothly as if in a lift. The whole circle was sinking into the building beneath it! The Aussies could see nothing as they descended into blackness, but they knew they were caught in a trap. Down and down they went, until eventually they came to a silent stop. Suddenly, searchlights blazed, banks of them all around, all focused on the Pom. The camper was perched on a rostrum, trapped in a circle of burning light. Jay Gee's hideous whisper seemed to fill the chamber.

'Welcome to America, Mr Pom!'

Chapter Fourteen

The Pom Comes Good

The lights dimmed and two double doors slid back, revealing Jay Gee Chicago behind an enormous desk.

'Nobody outsmarts Jay Gee Chicago. *I* put the white circle on the building – and you fell for it.' He gave a long wheezing laugh. 'Take 'em away!'

Ronnie and Reggie shoved the captured Aussies into Jay Gee's private cell. It was dark and dank and gloomy, fronted by heavy bars. Adelaide was already inside.

'You can't do this,' protested Sydney loudly. 'We're Australians!'

'And here is your room,' said Reggie, ignoring her. 'Hot and cold running water.'

'Down every wall!' said Ronnie. The Crows went off, cackling with laughter.

Adelaide looked severely at her would-be rescuers. 'You lot are as much use as a barbecue at a bush fire!'

'We tried, Addie,' said Darwin. 'We came to bring you back.'

'You couldn't bring a boomerang back!' she snorted.

'We crossed the Atlantic,' said Sydney indignantly.

'Risked life and limb,' said Frazer.

'And got caught!'

'Only a bit,' protested Darwin.

Adelaide looked round. 'Where's Bruce?'

'Hiding in the Pom,' said Frazer.

Adelaide unzipped her pouch and produced a little hacksaw.

'OK, Darwin, you start.'

'Start what, Addie?'

'Getting us out of here!'

Reluctantly Darwin started filing. It was a very thick bar

and a very small hacksaw. Even without his calculator, he reckoned it would take a good six months to saw through.

A voice said, 'Do you want a hand?'

'No thanks, I'll manage – ' Darwin looked up and saw Howard the Hyena leaning against the bars. Howard held out his paw. Guiltily, Darwin handed over the hacksaw.

'It's Darwin, isn't it?' said Howard silkily. 'Now, we mustn't damage other people's property – must we, Darwin, dear?'

Adelaide came to stand beside Darwin. 'He won't do it again,' she said apologetically.

'You promise?' trilled Howard.

Adelaide batted her eyelashes at him. 'Would I lie to my favourite hyena?'

Howard blushed. 'Your fav – hey, you're kidding me!'

'No Howard, I think you're just . . . Well, we all do.' She looked at the others. 'Don't we?'

Not really understanding, the others took their cue from Adelaide.

'Absolutely!' they chorused. 'We really do. Fair dinkum!'

'Can I have my saw back?' asked Adelaide gently.

Dazedly, Howard handed over the hacksaw. 'You know, I'm really surprised you feel like that. I mean, I haven't exactly been very nice to you, have I?'

'Oh, you've got your job to do,' said Adelaide understandingly.

'We don't hold it against you,' said Darwin.

'I wouldn't hold it anywhere near him,' muttered Sydney.

Adelaide was still laying on the flattery. 'I just don't know how Jay Gee would manage without you.'

Howard hung his head. 'Oh, I guess he'd find someone.'

'It just wouldn't be the same, Howie baby.'

Howard was almost weeping with gratitude. No one had ever been so nice to him before. No one had ever been nice to him at all, in fact.

'Oh you're all so kind, so understanding — ' he gushed.

'I know,' said Adelaide. 'Here, you couldn't get us some coffee, could you?'

Howard looked dubious. 'I'd love to, but I'm not supposed to leave you alone.'

'Oh, we won't tell anyone,' promised Sydney.

Howard looked at their happy smiling faces. 'Well, OK then! Cappuccino?'

Adelaide smiled. 'Cuppa anything!'

While the Aussies befriended Howard, the spotlit Pom stood alone on its rostrum, like a display model in some Motor Show for old wrecks. Ronnie and Reggie were bumbling about inside, searching for Bruce.

Ronnie clutched a fly swatter, Reggie a can of insecticide. They weren't having much luck.

'That spider's got to be in here somewhere,' said Reggie.

'What do we tell Jay Gee?' asked Ronnie.

They looked at each other. Then, both together, they said, 'Oh no!' as the sliding doors opened, and Jay Gee's desk and chair slid smoothly forwards. Reggie and Ronnie scrambled out of the Pom.

Bruce lifted the bonnet a few inches and peeped out. With a mad giggle he dropped out of sight.

Jay Gee glared at the Crows. 'You get that spider?' he rasped.

Reggie waved his swatter. 'Oh, yeah, flattened it, Jay Gee!'

Jay Gee waved a claw. 'OK, stronzos – scram!'

They scrammed.

Jay Gee's desk glided forward until he was beak to bonnet with the Pom. 'How do you like America?' he wheezed.

Silence.

'I asked you a question!' whispered Jay Gee menacingly.

More silence.

'Silence is not golden, my four-wheeled friend. You want I should take you for a ride?'

'Get knotted,' said the Pom deliberately.

Jay Gee chuckled. 'So you *can* talk!'

'What have you done with them Aussies?' demanded the Pom.

'Don't worry, Howard's taking care of them. Let's talk about us.'

The Pom looked blank. 'Eh?'

'You and me. Our relationship,' said the vulture.

'We don't 'ave one.'

Jay Gee looked admiringly at the Pom. 'You, my friend, are unique. A one-off!'

'Leave it out!' said the Pom awkwardly.

'Work for me and you can have anything you want!'

'You're kidding.'

Jay Gee leaned forward. 'A fuel-injected six-litre super-charged V-twelve engine generating four hundred brake horsepower . . .'

'I ain't gonna listen,' muttered the Pom feebly.

Jay Gee gestured widely with his claws. 'No longer the Winjin' Pom – *The American Dream!*'

The Pom couldn't help being impressed. 'Blimey!'

'You wanna think it over?'

'Yeah, well . . . what would you want me to do, pre-cisely?'

'A prison-break,' said Jay Gee airily. 'A few heists, a couple of kidnaps.'

'I wouldn't have to run anyone over?' asked the Pom cautiously.

'Come on, I got bulldozers for that. What d'ya say?'

The Pom wrestled with its conscience – and lost. 'OK, I'm in.'

Jay Gee was overjoyed. 'You'll never regret this, Pommy baby! Say, do you have any other gifts I ought to know about?'

'I can't think of anyfink . . . Arf a mo, there's me traffic warden trick. Now you see it, now you don't . . .'

Slowly the Pom faded into invisibility.

Jay Gee looked on in fascination as the Pom slowly became visible again. 'Mama mia! Now I see everything! We were made for each other. You get some rest, partner. OK? You got a busy day tomorrow!'

'OK, Jay Gee.'

Howard bustled into the cell with a trayful of coffee mugs. 'Hi, guys! Four cappuccinos! And I brought you some chocolate cookies!'

'Oh, we just love you, Howard,' said Sydney.

Howard found he couldn't open the cell door. He needed both hands for the tray. 'Oh, silly me!' He moved closer to the bars. 'Could you just get my key from my belt, Addie baby? It's the big one.'

Adelaide detached the key and opened the cell door. Howard came in with his tray and looked round. 'It's not my best china, but it'll have to do . . . Now, where shall I put the tray?'

There was a sudden clang.

Howard turned round to see the Aussies looking at him from the other side of the bars. Adelaide was just locking the door.

'Put the tray anywhere, Howard. Treat the place as your own,' she told him triumphantly.

'Mother told me never to trust a wallaby,' sobbed Howard.

The Aussies hurried away, and quickly made their way to the hangar where Jay Gee was keeping the Pom.

They opened the door and saw the Pom perched up on his rostrum.

'OK, let's get in!' whispered Adelaide.

They scuttled across the floor and Adelaide reached out to open the door. Suddenly spotlights flashed on and alarm bells clanged. The door slid back, and there was Jay Gee at his desk, Reggie and Ronnie behind him clutching machine-pistols.

'They was trying to get away, Jay Gee,' said the Pom virtuously.

'You winjin' creep, Pom!' yelled Adelaide. 'You couldn't sink any lower if your wheels fell off!'

'Goodbye, schmucks,' said Jay Gee.

Half an hour later, he was briefing his team on his master plan to spring Max Canary from gaol.

'OK, Howard,' he ordered.

'Ready when you are, Mr Chicago.' Howard switched on a projector.

'Number one, Calaboose State Penitentiary,' said Jay Gee. He sighed. 'Upside down . . .'

The Crows stifled their giggles. Howard put the slide in the right way up.

'OK, number two, the exercise yard.'

Another slide appeared – Howard in front of the Taj Mahal. Reggie and Ronnie spluttered hysterically.

'Schmuck!' hissed Jay Gee.

Howard put the right slide in the projector and they saw a diagram of a yard and the adjoining prison blocks.

'You land in the prison yard and make your way to C block. Max Canary's in cell thirteen. Unlucky for some, huh?'

Later that night, Reggie, Howard and Ronnie were crammed into the front seat of the Pom. They were back on the roof of the skyscraper. 'OK, Pom,' said Reggie. 'Time to go!'

The Pom started to vibrate. He shuddered, spread his stubby wings and drove off the edge of the building and up into the air, sweeping over the moonlit towers of Chicago.

In his office, Jay Gee snatched up a radio-mike. 'Jay Gee to Winjin' Pom. Jay Gee to Winjin' Pom . . .'

His voice crackled from Reggie's walkie-talkie.

'Yes, Jay Gee.'

'Synchronize your watches. The time is twenty-two hundred.'

Ronnie stared at his watch. 'Can't do mine.'

'Why not?' asked Reggie.

'Only goes up to twelve . . .'

As the Pom flew through the night sky he heard a little voice. Bruce was clinging to his front bumper.

'Pom?'

'Wot?'

'Jay Gee's sucked you in, ain't he? Got you doing his dirty work.'

'I am 'is partner,' said the Pom with dignity.

'Partner!' jeered Bruce. 'You're his gofer. Gofer this, gofer that. What about your mates? You couldn't care less, could ya?'

'Why should I – they're only Aussies.'

'Ya selfish old rust-bucket,' squeaked Bruce.

'What if I am?' returned the Pom.

'Jay Gee's gonna do 'em in,' said Bruce desperately. 'Don't that mean anything to yer?'

'There it is!' said Reggie. There were over the Penitentiary. As he swooped down, the Pom heard Bruce's words in his mind. *'He's gonna do 'em in! Doesn't that mean anything to ya?'* The Pom's conscience was giving him gyp. He hadn't actually betrayed the Aussies – Jay Gee's alarms had done that – but he'd been quick to line up with the winning side.

'OK, Pom,' said Reggie. 'Pom?'

'I heard ya the first time.'

'Stand by to disappear!'

The Pom dropped down into the exercise yard, landing with a bang.

'Disappear, Pom,' hissed Reggie. *'Disappear!'*

But the Pom didn't disappear. Instead he zoomed round the yard, flashing his headlights and blaring his horn.

'What's he up to?' yelled Ronnie. ''E's gone mad!' The radio in the dashboard lit up, blaring out 'Land of Hope and Glory' at full volume. Spotlights burst from the walls catching the Pom in circles of light.

'You clapped-out old pile of junk!' snarled Reggie.

'How could you do this to me?' sobbed Howard. 'How *could* you?'

'He's sewn us up,' said Ronnie indignantly.

Reggie sighed. 'The word is stitched – birdbrain!'

Suddenly the yard was full of heavily armed police pigs. A tannoy voice boomed, 'Come out with your hands up!'

'You heard 'im,' said the Pom. 'Out! And mind me paintwork!'

Howard and the Crows climbed out, and were promptly grabbed by guards. As they dragged him away Howard screamed, 'There's been a positively dreadful mistake!'

'And you made it, buddy!' growled the guard.

The Pom zoomed round in a circle and took off, roaring noisily away over the rooftops.

Back at Jay Gee's tower, the vulture was saying goodbye to his captives. Roped back to back in a neatly bound parcel, Adelaide, Frazer, Sydney and Darwin were dangling from a swivel fixed to a metal girder in his office. The end of the girder projected out through the open window.

Jay Gee was entertaining them with one last organ recital.

'Do you know you'll never get away with this?' yelled Adelaide.

'You hum it and I'll play it!' screamed Jay Gee with a burst of maniacal laughter.

A familiar rusty voice came from the intercom. 'Pom to Jay Gee, Pom to Jay Gee.'

Jay Gee snatched the mike. 'Pom? Where's Reggie?'

'The game's up, you evil old psychopath. I've turned 'em all in!'

'*Whaat?*' Jay Gee's claws hit the keyboard in a terrifying discord. He began cursing in Italian.

'See you in the funny farm, freako!' boomed the Pom's voice. 'Over and out!'

Dangling from their girder the Aussies were cheering.

'The Pom came good!' said Adelaide.

'He came very good,' said Darwin.

Only Sydney remembered their own position. 'Mother!' she shrieked. There was a hammering on the office door. 'Open up – police!'

Jay Gee swung round. 'Wait a minute – I *own* the police.' There was a brief pause. Then the voice said, 'Open up, police – *boss!*'

Jay Gee turned back to his Wurlitzer. 'And now, a little thing that goes something like this!'

Dramatic chords crashed from the organ – and the roped-up Aussies began moving along the girder. They crossed the office – and moved on out the window. They were dangling from a beam projecting from a skyscraper window, thousands of feet above the ground.

'I hate heights,' muttered Adelaide. More chords crashed from the office – and a little gadget that incorporated a circular saw began sliding along the beam. When it reached the rope . . .

'Not to mention mechanical saws,' she added sourly.

'What a way to end the innings,' sighed Frazer bravely.

The saw reached the rope . . . the fibres began to fray one by one . . . Seconds later the rope parted and the Aussies dropped . . .

. . . Only to land on something metallic, and invisible,

'What a way to end the innings.'

just below them. For a moment they just sat there in mid-air. Then, slowly the Pom re-materialized underneath them . . .

They were unbound, in the Pom, and flying home.

'What made you change your mind, Pom?' asked Adelaide.

'I dunno,' muttered the Pom. 'Bruce gimme a hard time.'

'Well done, Brucie,' said Frazer and the others added their congratulations.

Bruce was never averse to singing his own praises. 'Bruce Red-Back of Gullagaloona! The eight-legged wonder of the world!'

'And what about me, then?' moaned the Pom. 'Don't I get any thanks? Nobody gives a monkey's, do they? Always the same, pushed around and treated like dirt . . .'

'Stop winjin', Pom!' yelled the Aussies.

'I was not winjin',' said the Pom with offended dignity. 'I was just pointing out a few home truths.'

Still muttering and grumbling, the Winjin' Pom flew home to new adventures.